"I'm so sorry they got pulled into this. If I thought it would help, I'd go back to Chicago." She lifted her gaze to his. "It wouldn't help, would it?"

"He knows I'm involved, and he's not happy about it." Noah scooted closer to her and placed his hand on her knee. "Count on one thing—I won't leave your side until he's no longer a threat."

With a sad smile she covered his hand with hers. He couldn't look away from her green eyes. So much hurt, so much pain, and yet a determination buried deep that she couldn't hide. He turned his hand and squeezed hers, offering comfort.

She gnawed on her lip, her nerves showing through. He couldn't look away. The awareness that had been flickering through him since he'd seen her again erupted. He was so close to her, if he leaned over just a bit, their lips would touch.

If he ever kissed her, he didn't know if he'd be able to stop.

SECRET OBSESSION

ROBIN PERINI

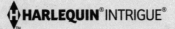

Recycling programs
for this product may
not exist in your area.

For my readers.

Thanks for the wonderful letters
telling me you loved the Bradford family
from *Finding Her Son*. Noah's story
exists because of you.

ISBN-13: 978-0-373-69779-3

SECRET OBSESSION

Printed in U.S.A.

ABOUT THE AUTHOR

Award-winning author Robin Perini's love of heart-stopping suspense and poignant romance, coupled with her adoration of high-tech weaponry and covert ops, encouraged her secret inner commando to take on the challenge of writing romantic suspense novels. Her mission's motto: "When danger and romance collide, no heart is safe."

Devoted to giving her readers fast-paced, high-stakes adventures with a love story sure to melt their hearts, Robin won a prestigious Romance Writers of America Golden Heart Award in 2011. By day she works for an advanced technology corporation, and in her spare time you might find her giving one of her many nationally acclaimed writing workshops or training in competitive small-bore-rifle silhouette shooting. Robin loves to interact with readers. You can catch her on her website, www.robinperini.com, and on several major social-networking sites, or write to her at P.O. Box 50472, Albuquerque, NM 87181-0472.

Books by Robin Perini

HARLEQUIN INTRIGUE
1340—FINDING HER SON
1362—COWBOY IN THE CROSSFIRE
1381—CHRISTMAS CONSPIRACY
1430—UNDERCOVER TEXAS
1465—THE CRADLE CONSPIRACY
1512—SECRET OBSESSION

CAST OF CHARACTERS

Lyssa Cafferty—Under WitSec protection, this sole survivor of a serial killer has a precious secret to guard. When the killer finds her, can she trust anyone, or will the man sent to save her also betray her?

Noah Bradford—When this ex-marine and deadly operative receives a call to protect the fiancée of his murdered best friend, can he guard Lyssa from a killer—and his heart from the woman he's loved from afar?

Archimedes—Infinity is his trademark. He's brilliant, vicious and determined, and his secret obsession is Lyssa.

Reid Nichols—The only person in WitSec Lyssa trusts. Has he betrayed her location to Archimedes?

Jack Holden—Lyssa's fiancé died at Archimedes's hands, saving her life. Can his best friend, Noah, stop the serial killer?

Rafe Vargas—Noah's trusted teammate has his own secrets. Will he lose more during this case than he ever imagined?

Covert Technology Confidential (CTC)—This organization of elite warriors helps those who have run out of options. But has the team met its match?

Chapter One

The sting of frozen rain pricked Lyssa Cafferty's cheeks, another attack she couldn't prevent. She hurried from the L station toward her small Chicago apartment. If only she could pull her hood over her head, duck down and avoid the piercing needles of ice on her face, but then she'd lose her peripheral vision.

She couldn't afford to allow comfort to trump safety.

Not now. Not ever.

Instead, she tugged her thrift-store winter coat tighter around her body, the jacket too big but at least warm. She peered over one shoulder then the other, seeing only commuters huddled against the winter wind and racing down Roger's Park streets. No one familiar.

She picked up her pace and pressed on through the blustery weather. Of course, she wouldn't recognize the man out to kill her until she was already dead.

Two years. Two long, horrible years since the night she'd lost Jack, since she'd lost her love, her life and everything that had made the world wonderful.

She couldn't have imagined things would get worse after Jack's murder.

They had.

A brilliant, uncatchable psycho had made it his business to find her.

Archimedes.

Just his name made her heart stutter…with fear and fury. He'd stolen her life.

She paused two blocks from her apartment and, ignoring the cold, stilled. On high alert, her entire body tensed. She struggled to calm the rapid beat of her heart.

Some days she just prayed he'd find her and get it over with. Those were the days when the constant state of fear wore down her soul.

Most days, though, she longed to look him in the eye and kill him for what he'd done to Jack, and to her. For the precious moments she'd lost with the one thing she loved more than herself. The one secret she'd die to protect.

She refused to even let her mind go there. She couldn't contemplate what might have been. Or what could be. Until Archimedes was brought to justice, this was her life. She had to focus on staying alive. At least for one more day.

Lyssa shifted, keeping her movements subtle, scanning each person, each darkened corner, searching for anything out of place, anyone following her. Her gaze flickered back and forth, furtive and cautious. He could be anyone, anywhere.

With each new stretch of building and street, her chest tightened in dreaded anticipation. She hurried past a couple of boarded-up storefronts and still, he wasn't there.

For three hundred and fifty-three days he hadn't been there.

One more day and he hadn't found her.

She tugged her hood lower and raced through the main entrance to her building. She trudged up the stairs, acutely aware of each squeak. A baby cried in apartment 219. At the sound, Lyssa paused, her hand instinctively reaching for the brass doorknob. A wave of despair nearly propelled her to her knees. A shush and a coo, and the baby quieted.

She squeezed her eyes shut against the burning wells in the corners. She couldn't think about the past, or her loss. She had to stay focused.

With careful placement of each step, she padded across the floor, knowing the location of each creak, a skill she worked to perfect every single day. She needed to move silently, invisibly.

Finally, she stopped in front of the small apartment the Justice Department had arranged for her. So-called Witness Security. She wasn't the best witness. She'd only heard the whispers of a madman, but had never seen him. And she certainly wasn't secure.

She was simply the sole survivor of a man who'd killed dozens.

The walnut door to her temporary home appeared exactly as she'd left it, down to the small slip of paper she'd wedged near the hinge. A trick she'd learned. Few would notice it, and as long as the paper didn't move, Lyssa could be confident no one had opened the door.

Safe at last.

She slipped the key into the dead bolt. As she tried to turn it, the key resisted in the lock ever so slightly. At the slight deviation from normal, she hesitated, her instincts firing.

The cold. It *could* be the cold. The temperature had plummeted twenty degrees today.

It probably *was* the cold.

One hand slipped into her pocket to the phone she carried with her. She hesitated. She couldn't call Gil again. She'd contacted her WitSec handler three times this month already. All false alarms.

The last time, after he'd rushed over to her place, she'd witnessed irritation in his eyes, though he'd tried to hide his reaction. He couldn't understand. She'd been in Chicago almost a year. Too long. She knew in her gut time was running out.

She flipped open her bag with her free hand and gripped the butt of the black-market .45 in her purse. Gil may have read the file, but he didn't comprehend the minute-by-minute fear that stalked her. Archimedes wasn't a typical serial killer. He was smart. He was thorough, and for some reason he had Lyssa in his sights.

Hand tight on the weapon, trigger finger ready, she shoved open the door and stepped across the threshold of a place she could never call home.

The coppery scent of blood strangled her belly.

Gil Masters lay on the ground, dead, in a pool of blood.

Archimedes had found her.

She forced herself to look at Gil's face. Someone had gouged out his eyes. Empty sockets stared unseeing at her, accusing. She didn't want to look lower, but she had to. His shirt had been ripped open, a frame for Archimedes's handiwork.

She froze, unable to look away from the horrifying, familiar symbol carved into his belly.

Infinity.

The curves of the sideways eight dripped with rivulets of blood streaking down his abdomen along his torso, pooling beneath him.

Archimedes had found her.

"No. God, no."

She lifted the gun and froze in place.

No sound. No movement. No creak of the floor.

No one was there.

She slowly turned, the muscles in her arms, legs and neck all at the ready.

Waiting.

Waiting for the attack to come out of nowhere. Waiting to die.

Each second became an hour. Each inch of movement felt like a mile.

But nothing happened. No heaving breaths, no hand over her mouth. No sadistic whisper in her ear.

She couldn't tell how many seconds had passed when she realized she wasn't going to die. At least not in this moment.

He really wasn't here.

But his message was.

She might not know what meaning infinity had for the killer, but she could read these words.

Blood smeared the wall, the promise indisputable.

No one will come between us. You will be mine.

Her gaze whipped around the apartment, her throat tightened in panic. What if he was watching, just waiting for her to let her guard down?

She had to get out.

She raced into her bedroom and grabbed the jewelry box from the top dresser drawer, digging through it until she pulled out a thin gold chain threaded through her diamond engagement ring. She slipped it around her neck.

Gil would have called her a fool. She didn't care. She wouldn't leave the ring behind.

A door slammed down the hall.

No more time. She yanked open her closet and grabbed a small duffel. The bag she kept packed. Always.

Lyssa heaved it over her shoulder and clutched the ring. "Help me, Jack."

She ran past Gil's body. Guilt pounded in her head. He had a family, a wife, two kids, five and seven years old. A girl and a boy. Witness and handler weren't supposed to get to know each other, but over a year, she had learned things about the man who watched out for her.

"I'm sorry. So sorry," she murmured. She closed her eyes in regret, tore down the stairs and hurried out of the apartment building. She wouldn't be coming back.

Speeding past end-of-the-day commuters, she tried to tame her panting breaths. She rushed up the stairs to the L platform and hopped onto the first southbound train. Her trembling legs refused to hold her. She sank into an empty seat.

The image of Gil's face, the void where his eyes should have been, battered into her memory. She'd never forget.

Lyssa clutched the duffel to her. She had to push Gil aside, cold and heartless as that was. She had to concentrate. She had to survive.

The train rumbled beneath her, the iron supports whizzing past, each second taking her farther from the body of the man who had sworn to protect her, further from the life she'd lived for almost a year.

She knew one thing; this wouldn't be a repeat of the last time Archimedes had found her. This time *she* would dictate the rules.

She caught sight of an ad for the Atrium Mall from the train's window. A lot of people. Open late.

She had no idea how much time had passed when she walked into the huge shopping center. Crowds milled around her. She let herself breathe again. Archimedes didn't kill in public. Or he hadn't yet. She found a corner table in the food court, near a wall, out of the way. She shoved her hand into her pocket and grabbed the unused, prepaid cell phone.

She dialed but couldn't stop her hands from shaking. She hated the response, hated the show of vulnerability.

Somewhere inside she had to find the strength to do what two years ago she could never have imagined doing.

She didn't bother with 911. They couldn't help.

She dialed a number she'd memorized a year ago.

"Nichols," the voice barked.

The one man she trusted not to betray her.

"He found me again."

NOAH BRADFORD VAULTED onto the edge of the roof from the ladder propped against his father's house. The brisk morning air would make it easy to stay alert. He scaled the pitched tile using techniques not so different from an escape he'd engineered in Kazakhstan. At least this time bullets weren't flying past his head.

Donning an elaborate tool belt stuffed with everything from levels to screwdrivers to ratchets and hammers, his brother Chase followed Noah to the satellite system.

Noah knelt to inspect the latest winter storm's hail damage. "Colorado weather is *not* kind to my toys," he muttered. "No wonder Dad's had so many outages."

Ignoring the fact that he should have found time to repair this months ago, Noah grabbed a small set of tools from his back pocket and quickly adjusted the encryption device while Chase checked out the damaged tiles from the storm.

They'd almost finished before Chase spoke. "You were out of touch for over a month, bro," he accused. "Dad was worried."

Yet another way Noah had let down his dad. He sent Chase a sidelong glance. "I told you, I had business—"

"You gave the family a cock-and-bull story that even a child would see through. We're not stupid, Noah. Dad developed pneumonia two weeks ago. We couldn't get ahold of you. You didn't answer your cell. No one from your companies could tell us anything. Not acceptable."

A small screwdriver fell from Noah's normally secure grip, rolled down the roof and tumbled over the side. He let out a sharp curse before snapping the cover over the panel. "I can't talk about it."

He eased to the edge and made his way down the ladder in seconds. Chase followed. "I'm just giving you fair warning. You won't be able to avoid the truth this time. Dad's staging an intervention."

Noah stilled, the muscles at the base of his neck tying into a familiar knot. He looked over at his SUV. He could just leave. His family was better off not knowing about his side job as the Falcon. They knew about his public career. The encryption and software patents he'd developed as a teenager had turned into big business. They'd never understood why he'd left it and home at eighteen for the Marines.

They definitely had no idea that he now worked for an organization that took on tasks the government or military couldn't risk.

Chase slapped his brother's shoulder and the move yanked Noah from the dark memories.

"Come clean," his brother said. "Just like you did when Dad caught you and Mitch sneaking out during high school. Some things aren't worth avoiding."

"And sometimes the truth doesn't make it better," Noah said. "This isn't high school."

Bracing himself, he entered his father's home, past the handicapped ramp that his siblings, Mitch, Chase and Sierra, had installed. Noah had been on a job. By the time he'd returned, all he'd been able to do was write a check.

His mind already searching for a means of escape, he found his way into the living room. "Satellite is fixed.

You've got TV and internet, all encrypted for your super-secret-police consulting."

His father didn't take the bait. Paul Bradford said nothing; he simply quirked an eyebrow while the football game played in the background. Noah squirmed under his dad's focus. He might be in a wheelchair after a gunshot severed his spinal cord, but nothing was wrong with his instincts.

Noah's forefinger scratched at his knuckle. "What?"

His brother Chase shrugged and passed him a longneck bottle with that I-told-you look.

Paul Bradford drummed his fingers on his chair. "I did a little digging—"

Noah's hand paused on the way to his mouth, then he took a long gulp. Yeah, he'd been brilliant encouraging his father's interest in computers. Noah knew exactly how he inherited his own tech ability. The idea of setting Dad up with a side business doing investigations had seemed like a perfect way to keep Paul Bradford engaged in life—and law enforcement. Noah downed half the bottle, the cool liquid sliding down his throat. What a fool. "Your point?"

"I hit a damn brick wall," Paul growled.

At least something had gone right today.

"You want to tell me why I can't find out anything about you, Noah? Short of the vanilla bio you published on the websites of your companies." Paul rolled his chair across the wooden floor, coming a few inches from Noah. "I haven't pried into your life before. Well, that stops now. Exactly what are you into, Noah? How worried should we be?"

His sister, Sierra, saved him from answering. For the moment. She exited the kitchen with a large tray of chips and guacamole, followed by Mitch and his very pregnant wife, Emily. Mitch held Emily's two-year-old son Joshua in his arms while Emily waddled into the living room and settled down on a hard-back chair with a sigh. "I can't get out of that sofa," she said with a smile. "Last time, Mitch had to use a crane to hoist me."

Thankful for something to do—anything to avoid answering questions—Noah doled out a plate for Emily. She looked at him in surprise. "Thank you?"

"It's not like our resident man-of-mystery has learned manners," Chase commented. "He's just avoiding Dad's questions."

Noah winced and eyed the door. He should go. This conversation had already strayed too close to truths he couldn't discuss—some classified, some, well, they'd just worry. Some—things he'd done he would never talk about. To anyone.

He tugged on his jacket. "I'd better go."

Before he could get to the door, Emily gripped Noah's hand and her sympathetic gaze met his. He really loved his sister-in-law. She saw through more than most. Probably because she'd been to hell and back. "They're worried about you, Noah. You scared them this time. Your dad, too," she mouthed the last few words.

Noah scrubbed his hand over his face. His dad had lost weight from the illness. He looked pale. "I've made sure you can reach me anytime, anywhere," he said, tugging a card from his wallet and handing it to his father. "This number will page me no matter where I am. I designed it myself. I won't be out of touch again."

Paul tucked the card into his shirt pocket. "It's not about that, Noah. It's about the riddle your life has become. What if something had happened to you? How would we ever know?"

"I'm a trained marine. I can take care of myself on a business trip."

"Business trip, my butt," Sierra said under her breath.

"You haven't shown your face at any of your companies in six months," Chase said. "Just a few conference calls. So where have you been?"

That they'd infiltrated the careful web he and Crystal had set up gave him pause. He had some major shoring up to do once he figured a way out of this mess.

Mitch settled next to Emily, clasping her hand while he bounced Joshua on his knee. "We get that you like your privacy, Noah. You've always preferred hiding off in your lab with your electronics and computers, but this is different. No word. Not even an answer to the calls and emails when Dad was in the hospital."

Truth was, they didn't know him at all. Noah had never wanted to disappear, but he hadn't fit in. He'd never fit in. Mitch and Chase were the athletes and Sierra was the perfect daughter. They hadn't understood him. Noah kneaded his neck. That's why he'd joined the Marines, hoping to find a place in the family. But then the secrets just got worse. He couldn't talk about his job. Or the Falcon.

So, most of the time, he didn't talk. He just listened. Even now, how could he tell his family that he'd spent the past six months dealing with one crisis after another for Covert Technology Confidential based in the middle-of-nowhere Carder, Texas?

He'd backed off the government intel jobs, but CTC kept him busy, and truth be known, not a lot safer.

His phone vibrated in his pocket. He slipped it from his coat and glanced at the number. A number he hadn't seen in a very long time. "We'll have to talk about this later," he said. "There's an emergency in Phoenix…" He let his voice trail off, too tired to lie. He sighed. "There's an emergency. Let's leave it at that."

"Someday you'll have to trust us with what's going on

in your life, son," Paul said quietly. "We're your family. We love you. We want to know you."

Noah looked at them. They did love him. He knew that. He just...he didn't know if they'd like him very much after the choices he'd been forced to make. Even with his brother Mitch and his dad as cops, would his family understand what the Falcon had been forced to do to save his own life and, more importantly, the lives of his men. Not knowing was better.

"See you soon," he said. Emily struggled to her feet and hugged him close. "Be careful," she said softly.

His throat constricted and he walked out to the front porch, the brisk winter air freezing his ears. He flicked on the receiver. "I'm surprised to hear from you, Reid. It's been almost eighteen months. What happened to in-communicado?"

"I'll call you back," his old marine buddy said. "Stand by."

He'd known Reid since basic training, and only twice had his voice held that much tension. Noah's posture went rigid. This couldn't be good.

The phone rang again. This time the screen showed an unknown number. Noah flicked a switch on the side of the phone. A Washington, D.C., number popped onto the screen. "What the hell's going on?"

"Archimedes found her," Reid said.

Reid didn't have to say any more. Noah closed his eyes. Jack's fiancée, Alessandra Cummings. The moment Jack had introduced her, Noah had been in awe. She was open, transparent and full of joy. She'd accepted Jack for who he was, for what he'd done. What would it feel like to be loved as much as Alessandra had loved Jack? Not a day went by when Noah hadn't wondered. Damn, Jack had been lucky. For a year or so, he and Alessandra had lived a fairy tale. Until Archimedes.

It had been two years since Jack's death. Noah didn't know what name she used now. He'd promised Reid he wouldn't track her after Archimedes had found her just a few months into hiding. To keep her safe, Noah had agreed.

"Is she…" He didn't want to finish the question.

"She's still alive as of an hour ago." Reid paused. "This is the third time he's located her, Noah. She should be dead. For whatever reason, he hasn't killed her, but I have a leak at Justice. I need your help."

Noah glanced at his watch. "I can leave within the hour. Where is she?"

"We placed her in Chicago. She's ditched her phone. She'll call me at noon. She's scared, but it's more than that. I don't like the sound of her voice. She's on the edge."

"Has she given up?"

"I don't think so, but she's tired of waiting. Hell, so am I. The guy's a damn ghost." Noah could hear the fatigue in his friend's voice. "I should have called last night, but I'd hoped the news would be better."

"How close are you to catching him?" Noah asked. "Straight up."

"No closer than the night Jack died."

Noah ground his teeth together. He should have insisted he stay on the case.

"Archimedes is better than good. I reviewed the current status of the investigation after she called last night. They can't nail him down. He doesn't leave evidence behind when he kills. Hell, half the time I think they're pinning all unsolved murders with little or no evidence on him."

Noah tugged the keys from his jeans and strode to his SUV. "We both owe Jack our lives. This time, we protect her. And we find Archimedes."

LYSSA SAT INSIDE the public library hidden by some shelves but with a clear view of the front entrance. She clutched her new phone in her hand. She'd transferred from train to train all night long, switching lines and directions. She couldn't keep up this pace much longer. Plus she didn't have an unlimited supply of funds, just the one thousand dollars she'd scrimped and saved and placed in the pocket of her ready bag.

She hated to admit she'd been stupid yesterday. She'd been thinking about the moment Archimedes would find her for a year, and when it happened, panic had won. She'd run.

In the clear light of day—and without Gil's body on the floor—logic ruled. She sat here, watching people go about their everyday lives, and realized this was the answer. The strategy.

Go on with her life. Keep doing what she'd been doing.

Let Archimedes find her.

It was a good plan. She couldn't go on any longer waiting to die. Archimedes was too smart, too deadly. She had too much to protect, and if he ever discovered that her true vulnerability wasn't fear…she couldn't bear the thought.

A shiver of awareness registered at the back of her neck. She swallowed. Had he found her already?

Her attention shifted to the entrance of the library. She peered at a tall figure pushing through the double doors. He wore jeans, a leather bomber jacket and cowboy boots. He didn't belong in a library.

But she recognized the shape of his face, the color of his hair, and surprisingly enough, the fit of his jeans.

Where had that come from? She'd only met him three times. Once at a barbecue with Jack, once in a crowded bar and once at Jack's funeral.

He scanned the room, then paused when his gaze fell

on her. She shifted in her chair. Would he know her? He didn't hesitate. He walked over.

"Alessandra," he said quietly, his deep voice washing over her.

"Lyssa," she whispered.

He nodded and surveyed the room. "Let's switch locations before we talk."

She ducked her head and grabbed the small bag.

"That's all you have?"

"I'm traveling light these days."

His brown eyes darkened. "You'll be safe soon."

Lyssa let him lead her out of the library and down the street half a block. When they passed a small alley, she pulled him into the shadow between the two buildings. She glanced around, but they were alone, save for a trash bin and a stash of cardboard boxes, blankets and empty whiskey bottles.

"What's this about?" He frowned down at her, shifting so she remained hidden from the street by his large frame.

"I don't want to be safe, Noah. I agreed for Reid to bring you in because Jack told me you were the smartest person he'd ever met. And you were ruthless. I want to find Archimedes, Noah. And I want him dead."

THE DINER WAS dingy, grimy and dirty. He pulled a handkerchief from his pocket and wiped the chair down before carefully sitting in the booth.

Alessandra had run, but he would have her. Soon.

He shifted in his seat. His feet clung to the sticky floor and he grimaced. Carefully using two fingers, he opened the menu then couldn't bear to hold the germ-infested plastic in his hands. He rubbed the table with two napkins to protect his skin from touching the filth.

"Are you going to order or keep cleaning?" A young

woman with streaked blue hair and a tattoo on her neck stared down at him, chomping her gum.

He focused on the table, gripping his trousers. She was rude, but she was probably rude to everyone. He should ignore the urge. He had more important work to do.

"Come on, buddy. Either order or get out. I ain't got all day."

He pasted a smile on his face, but inside, his head throbbed, pounding at his temples. "Coffee. Three sugars. Cream. Not creamer, cream. The kind that comes from cows."

"Freak," she muttered and snagged the menu from him.

He clenched his fists and watched with an irritated gaze as she grabbed a cup, poured coffee into it and carelessly dumped in nondairy creamer.

As if he couldn't tell.

The waitress practically dropped the cup on the table. Coffee sloshed over the edge. She didn't even bother to wipe it down. She sashayed away to another booth where a smiling young man winked at her.

They ignored him. They always ignored him.

She wouldn't ignore him for long.

Abandoning the coffee, he stood and walked out the door. He took a half dozen steps and waited, an alley situated strategically behind him.

The girl ran out of the coffee shop. "You can't leave without paying!" she shouted.

"And you need to learn some manners."

He smiled and grabbed her neck in a calculated pressure, using twenty pounds per square inch directed at her carotid artery. He wanted her weak, not unconscious.

He dragged her behind an industrial waste bin out of sight. Car horns honked, but no one saw. They ignored. Everything. Everyone.

Her eyes grew wide. She whimpered, trying to break his hold.

"I don't think so, girl." With a smile, he slipped a knife from his pocket. "You're very rude," he whispered, pressing the knife against her side. "You must be taught a lesson." With a quiet move he slit her shirt on the side and flicked the sharp knife through a layer of skin.

She opened her mouth, but before she could scream he covered her lips with his hand. He pressed her against the brick wall. "I won't be ignored," he said softy. "Or dismissed." He drew the knife around her torso, positioned the blade between her ribs and shoved it in.

She tried to scream, tried to bite him. "Don't bother," he said softly. "You're bleeding inside. You'll be dead soon."

The waitress tried to shake her head, then she blinked. Life faded from her eyes. He let her drop to the ground.

With practiced ease he slid his knife through her dress, baring her chest. He didn't look on her tattooed curves with desire. Just disgust.

He dragged his blade across the tainted pale skin of her belly, then stopped. She wasn't worthy of him or his attention. Marred with drawings and piercings.

Alessandra Cummings had none of those. Alessandra Cummings was perfect.

She'd run from him, though.

What a disappointment. He'd forgiven her the slight twice before, but this time she would have to prove herself worthy of him.

If she didn't pass the test…

She would. She would come to understand they belonged together. Had always belonged together. Just the two of them.

He stared down at the woman's body, then at his hands, bloody and uncovered. He tugged out a vial from his

pocket and sprinkled the body with the concentrated accelerant he'd created.

The strike of a match and her body was engulfed in
flames. He tugged his coat's cashmere collar around his
neck and slipped down the alley before rounding the corner.

Behind him someone shouted.

Sirens screamed, but he didn't care.

Archimedes had a seduction to plan.

Chapter Two

In the midday light, the Chicago skyscrapers cast a shadow, smothering the alley with pockets of darkness. Noah studied Lyssa: her unwavering gaze, the determined set of her jaw, the circles beneath her eyes and her furtive glance at every hiding place, as if waiting for Archimedes to leap out at her.

"You're exhausted—" he started.

"Weary to the bone," she said, "but not too tired to know what I have to do."

Fatigue written on her pale face, she stepped into the light. The sun illuminated the small worry lines in her forehead. She'd changed so much. He hated seeing her this way. He wanted to wrap her in his arms, comfort her and take the pain away. He wanted to tell her everything would be fine.

It would be a lie, though. He knew the truth and so did she. Archimedes had found her three times. He would find her again eventually. Unless Noah stopped him.

"Are you going to help me kill him or not?"

She didn't back down, but Noah recognized the edge she teetered on. He'd been there. On every mission. The adrenaline rush that kept you going for a while—until you crashed, or made a mistake.

His plan to hide Lyssa away and then go after the serial

killer himself exploded with the destruction of a rocket-propelled grenade. This was not the woman he'd met two years ago, the woman he'd envied his best friend over. The woman whose fluency in five languages intrigued him, whose nomadic childhood had shaped her desire to create a home with Jack. The joyously open woman for whom his friend had decided to give up fieldwork and take a desk job.

The woman Noah had fallen for before he'd realized how Jack felt about her.

No, he wouldn't go there. The woman standing before him had been through hell.

Noah knew the place well.

"Lyssa—" he began, not quite sure how—or if—he could convince her to stay at the safe house.

"Don't bother trying to convince me otherwise, Noah. I'm sick of being afraid," she said. "I'm done with running from a man no one can catch."

Her green eyes flashed with an emotion he couldn't pin down.

She finally sighed and raised her chin in steadfast resolve. "I'm tired of waiting to die."

"I won't let that happen." Noah took a step toward her but she shook her head. He paused, then lowered the arm he'd reached out.

"Don't make promises you can't keep, Noah. WitSec promised. Reid promised. The only person keeping his promise is Archimedes." She shifted her bag on her shoulder. "I *will* find Archimedes. You can help me or I'll go on my own. Either way, I'm finished postponing the inevitable. It will be over soon."

Noah didn't doubt her resolve for an instant, evoking a shot of admiration he hadn't expected. Lyssa had turned into a warrior, and damn if he didn't like her. A lot. Unfortunately, all that fire and vinegar would make his job a hell of a lot more complicated.

On so many levels.

If he'd met her in the field, he'd have been hard-pressed to keep his hands off her. He could imagine nights under the stars, working off the adrenaline of the mission in a too-small sleeping bag, hot, sweaty and satisfying.

As it was, she was Jack's fiancée—even if his friend was dead. That meant hands off.

"Fine. I'm on my own." Straightening her shoulders, she hesitated for a moment, peered up and down the street and the sidewalk, then took a step out of the alley.

What was she doing? He gripped her arm and pulled her into the protection of the building. Cornering her against the brick wall, he placed a hand next to her ear. "Hold on, Ally. I didn't say I wouldn't help you."

With only an inch between them, he could feel the slight tremble rush through her. A crackle of awareness vibrated between them. He'd never risked being this close to her and he fought his body's immediate response. He breathed in deeply, taking in the scent of lavender, then clenched his fist to stop himself from touching her caramel-colored hair. He stared down at her and her eyes widened, her pupils dilated, her emerald eyes sparked in response.

This was not good, but he couldn't deny the truth. Even strained to the limit, she was breathtaking. And he wanted her. He'd always wanted her.

With a shake of her head, she pressed her hands against his chest. He didn't move. He didn't want her taking off again. If he was going to protect her, he had to make her see her vulnerability. "Ally—"

"Don't call me that," she hissed, and with a quick, evasive move, ducked beneath his arm.

"Lyssa then," he corrected, turning slowly. "Impressive.

You've had self-defense training." He leaned closer, deliberately crowding her. "So, what's your plan to find Archimedes?"

"He wants me," she said, her voice matter-of-fact. "It's the one pattern I can predict. Unlike Reid and the Justice Department, I'm willing to use it. But this time on my terms."

"Become bait?" He studied her, from her eyes to her guarded stance. He recognized another layer of emotion in every pore of her body. Resignation. She was ready to die. Well, he wouldn't let it happen. "Do you have a weapon?" he challenged.

She opened her purse. ".45 caliber, hollow point ammo. Got it on the black market. Untraceable. Not that I care."

"Kimber 1911. A .45's got quite a kick."

"I spend hours every week on the range and at the gym. I can handle it. I like the rear sight. Besides, it'll blow a hole in him." Her eyes went frosty. "He won't get up again.

"If he comes to my apartment while I'm there, I have a super-shorty 12-gauge shotgun." She sent a pointed glance at the small ready bag at her feet.

He hadn't seen this spine of steel in her two years before, but he'd learned over time you didn't really know a person until they had their back against the wall. Jack had probably known Lyssa was a fighter, but she definitely had more guts than Noah had imagined.

"The WitSec marshal was armed, and he had more training and experience," Noah said, his voice soft and low. "Archimedes killed him. What makes you think you can do better?"

She clutched her purse—and the weapon—closer, but a flash of regret marred her expression before she shoved it away. She hadn't perfected cloaking her emotions the way Noah had. She'd learned to quell them, though. Noah hated she'd been forced to use the skill. His ability to turn off his feelings made him doubt his humanity sometimes. It also gave him the ability to think on his feet. Lyssa had thrown him a curve. He'd have to adjust.

"How long have you been planning to go after him?" he asked.

"Since Reid brought me to Chicago. I knew if the FBI couldn't locate him and put a case together, he'd eventually find me. I can't risk…"

She swiped her hand down her face.

"Risk what?" Noah asked, watching as her face turned to stone before she averted her gaze. Noah's instincts pinged a warning, that gut feeling that had kept him alive all these years. Every time he'd ignored the signs, he and his men had paid a heavy price. She was hiding something from him. Something important. "You're taking a huge chance pulling out of WitSec. They have resources. Why are you *really* doing this, Lyssa?"

She zipped her purse and lifted her duffel to her shoulder. "WitSec failed Gil. And me. If I stay in the program, I'll die anyway. Isn't that enough reason?"

Her gaze shifted to the left. Why was she lying? He was here to help. He lifted the bag from her shoulder and his hand brushed her skin. The touch made his nerves tingle. He wanted to pull her close but he couldn't. She was Jack's. Instead, he shoved the urge aside and shouldered the duffel. "Reid wants you safe."

"If he told you to hide me, just go home." She reached out a hand for her things. "I won't fight you *and* Archimedes. I can't."

Noah gripped the straps tighter. "Jack wouldn't want you to die, Lyssa."

Her arm dropped and she stumbled back as if he'd

punched her. Noah refused to regret the words. Some-times the end justified the means. He *would* keep her alive.

He owed Jack.

She swiped at her eyes, then blinked. "That was a cheap shot."

"Did it work?"

She studied him, crossing her arms, feet apart, ready for battle. "Okay, Mr. Hotshot Spy Guy, what would *you* do? According to Reid, the FBI task force has no leads. Even when only Reid and Gil knew my location, Archi-medes found me. He killed Gil and left me a message—"

"What message?" Noah interrupted. "Reid didn't men-tion a message."

"He wants me to be his. It was painted on my wall. In Gil's blood."

Her expression had frozen like stone, but Noah could see the effort in maintaining control. First the muscle at the base of her neck twitched, then her teeth bit into her lip. Finally, her shoulders slumped as if the energy required to keep up the front collapsed.

"No…no one else will d-die—" her voice broke "—because of me."

Here was a glimpse of the woman who cared, the woman Jack had fallen for, who wore her emotions for all to see. She might try to put up walls, be a cold-blooded vigilante, but even Lyssa couldn't keep her soft heart solid all the time.

Noah scratched his chin in resignation, the stubbly new beard not quite grown in yet. He'd thought he'd be head-ing back to Afghanistan before this call. "If I put you in a safe house, you won't stay, will you?"

"He'd find me," she said flatly. "So, what's the point?"

Noah slipped his secure phone from his pocket. "If we do this, we need help. Right now Archimedes has the upper hand. We don't know who's giving him information or how he's getting it."

Lyssa grabbed his arm. "I told you. There's a leak."

"I'm not calling WitSec or even the higher-ups in the Justice Department," he assured her. "Covert Technology Confidential is different. CTC isn't government. Highly paid, highly screened. I've put my life in their hands more than once."

She tugged at a gold chain around her neck. "I don't know…"

"Lyssa, look at me."

He wanted to see her face. He had to convince her.

She lifted her chin and those green eyes met his gaze with an unflinching challenge.

"I'm good at what I do, Lyssa. So are the people I work with. We can find Archimedes. We can take him." He clasped her shoulders, slid his hands to her elbows, down her arms, then squeezed her ice-cold fingers. "Jack trusted me. So can you."

She swallowed, and the gulp echoed between them. She looked down at the bag holding her weapon. One breath. Two breaths.

Had he persuaded her? He had this one chance. If she didn't choose to go with him, he'd have to do something he really didn't want to do—take her to the safe house against her will. He prayed she'd put her faith in him.

"Jack trusted you," she said finally. "I'll give you a chance, but if I get bad vibes, I won't say goodbye. I'll just disappear."

"And I'll be chasing after you until this is over."

Noah let one of Lyssa's hands go and dialed a number on the cell phone.

"Falcon?" the familiar voice answered through the phone. "Surprised to hear from you."

Ransom Grainger, the head of CTC—formerly known as Hunter Graham, formerly known as Clay Griffin and a dozen other aliases—used Noah's code name casually.

"Pretty good," Noah said. "How'd you know it was me. This phone is secure."

"Not from Zane." Grainger chuckled. "It's a good thing he's on our side…. What are you doing in Chicago?"

"I need a favor," Noah said, ignoring further proof of CTC's tracking prowess. He'd need every advantage. "It's a big one."

"Name it."

Lyssa pulled from his grip. Noah tried not to consider the loss of her touch. When she tugged at her bag, he slid it from her shoulder. She walked across the alley, crouched down and rummaged through her purse. She didn't fool Noah. She listened intently to every word he said. One misstep and she'd take off.

"I need a full team. We may have to tap into WitSec. Maybe even an FBI task force."

Grainger let out a low whistle. "I've got an insider—"

"No good. I have it from a top-notch source there's a leak."

A low whistle escaped from Grainger. "That'll be harder," he said, "but it can be done. You know better than anyone how to circumvent—"

"It's Archimedes."

At the mention of the serial killer's name, Lyssa's fingers fumbled momentarily at the duffel's zipper, then she shook it off. She yanked a sheath from the bag, followed by a knife. Noah couldn't take his eyes off her. With practiced moves she attached the weapon to her ankle. God, she had guts.

Grainger went silent. "What are you into, Noah? That

guy makes some of our intelligence operatives look like amateurs."

"Long story. I'm standing across the alley from the only woman to survive an attack by Archimedes. She needs help. He's found her. Again."

Lyssa didn't pause this time. She removed her ragged coat, slipped on a shoulder holster and fitted the oversize garment over the weapon. Yeah, she definitely knew her way around a firearm.

He understood the move. She'd decided to give him a bit of room, but she wasn't trusting anyone with her safety—not him, not CTC. She had armed herself with easy access to the .45 and her knife.

"What do you need?" Grainger asked. "Safe house?"

"She wants to track him down and eliminate him." Noah lowered his voice. "She wants to be bait."

The sound of drumming fingertips filtered through the phone. "It's risky."

"I know." Noah said. "If you can't do it—"

"I didn't say that. If half of the murders they've assigned to him are true, he needs exterminating. I'll pull Rafe, Zane and Elijah." Grainger paused and Noah could almost hear the man he had once called partner thinking through every conversation they'd ever had. "She must be important."

Noah's memories of a flag-draped coffin lingered in his mind, of the woman broken and sobbing, struggling to remain standing. No comparison to the warrior she had become. "She is."

"Expect the team in a few hours at Chicago Executive Airport. Elijah will want a firsthand look at the crime scene." Grainger let out a long, slow breath. "You want this done so the feds can prosecute?"

"Not necessarily," Noah said as he took in Lyssa's strained features. "I want her safe."

"You got it. No rules."

Grainger hung up, and Noah pocketed his cell. He faced Lyssa. "They'll be here soon."

"You trust them?"

"They're smart, savvy and won't run from a fight," Noah said. "And they've saved my life more than once. Kind of like Jack."

She shoved her hands into the pockets of her wool coat. "I can't afford to pay you," she said. "Everything I made while in WitSec has gone to training and weapons."

"I owe Jack my life." Noah gritted his teeth until his jaw ached. When he, Jack and Reid had started out in the Marines together, they'd covered each other's backs. That had never changed. Once Jack proposed to Lyssa, he'd taken a job stateside. Supposedly safe, to live out his life with Lyssa. He wasn't supposed to die at the hands of a madman in his own home. Noah would keep that oath. He'd cover Jack's back this time. "The last thing you need to worry about is money."

"Thank you."

"Thank me when Archimedes is behind bars."

"Or dead," Lyssa said, her gaze pointed. She pulled a piece of paper out of her bag. "Since Archimedes is obviously in Chicago and found my apartment, we should—"

Noah lifted his hand. "Hold on. You may have had an idea how you want to run this operation, but I'm in charge now. Archimedes has the upper hand at the moment. I want to put him off balance. We do this my way, Lyssa. I tell you when to run, to duck, to jump. I don't want an argument. We're switching up the game."

Lyssa frowned at him. "I let Gil pick my location, set up the meetings. Look what happened to him."

"I'm better than WitSec. So is my team." Noah crossed his arms. He'd do anything to keep her safe, even risk her anger. As long as she didn't run, they had a chance. "Are we in agreement?"

She paused, chewing on her lip. "I keep my weapons?"

Noah nodded.

"If we're not in immediate danger, then I want input. You'll listen?"

Damn, she was tenacious. He liked that about her, so he told her the truth. "You know Archimedes better than anyone. I'd be a fool not to take advantage. But I also know a few things about strategy and egomaniacal killers. I get final say."

Lyssa studied him, her green eyes intelligent and thoughtful. "I won't stay if I think we're losing ground. I won't spend another year in hiding. I just can't."

There it was, that small break in her voice, the vulnerability that clutched his heart and squeezed it into submission. He couldn't afford his emotions to take over, and yet he couldn't stop himself from these strange feelings that bubbled inside. He shoved the distraction away.

"CTC is bringing in a forensics expert, a computer tracker and…muscle. We'll finish the job."

"And what will *you* do, Noah? Besides try to take over."

"Me?" He pulled out a small coin and handed it to her. "I play with toys. Put it in your pocket. Keep it with you day and night."

She stared at what looked like a quarter and held it in her hand, giving him a suspicious glance. "Why give me a quarter?"

"It's a tracking device. Pretty much unlimited distance. I want to know where you are at all times."

"So, if Archimedes takes me and kills me, you'll find my body," she stated flatly.

Noah clasped her arms, the cheap wool coat scratchy under his palms. He pulled her to him. "Where's your faith, Lyssa? You showed me enough bravado to go after him. Now you have help. The best there is. We're not going to fail you. We'll keep you safe."

"Jack believed he could protect me from anything. He was trained. Archimedes killed him."

She shook her head, her gaze falling to the ground. "That psycho found me even when they removed my case from local jurisdiction and took it to the D.C. office. As much as I want to, I can't believe in you, Noah." She lifted her chin, her gaze unwavering and honest. "I can't afford to believe in anyone."

Chapter Three

Darkness had fallen over the city. More shadows, more hiding places. Lyssa crouched in the alleyway across from her apartment, four men at her back. They'd been waiting here over an hour. The temperature had dropped even more. Her fingers twitched. She pulled the coat tighter around her but couldn't stop the shiver.

"Here," Noah said, wrapping a soft scarf around her neck and rubbing his hands over her arms. "We'll get you someplace warm soon."

"No police," Rafe Vargas commented from his position just behind them.

She peered over her shoulder. The former Green Beret looked as if he could kill without caring—not unlike Archimedes—except Rafe's expression wasn't crazy; it was tortured. The patch over his left eye gave him the look of a pirate, but something in his expression when he'd exited the private plane and taken her hand in his had made Lyssa pause. He wasn't a killing machine. He was a man who did what he had to do. All these CTC operatives seemed to share that trait.

For the first time in a long time she wondered if they had a chance to get Archimedes.

"Reid is as good as his word," Noah said. "He'll call in

the murder tonight. Until then, we have unfettered access to the crime scene."

"He could get fired for not reporting," Zane Westin murmured behind them. "Especially since it's Archimedes." The operative specialized in electronic surveillance, but his bulk made Lyssa wonder at his other skills. He looked nearly as dangerous as Rafe.

"It'll be obvious the body has been there for twenty-four hours," Elijah interjected. The forensics expert carried some sort of large case. "Even the county medical examiner could figure that out based on core body temp, much less the FBI task force." He snapped on his gloves. "When can I get inside?"

"Reid should be here by now," Noah muttered, glancing at his watch.

Narrow lines of worry deepened between his brows causing prickles of alarm to raise on Lyssa's arms.

Behind her, Rafe, or *the enforcer* as she'd come to think of him, adjusted his eye patch. "Maybe the leak has him running cautious."

"Could be." Noah checked his phone again.

The streets had grown quieter; rush hour had ended. Lyssa shifted her position again. The men remained completely still, as if they were used to waiting endlessly. She couldn't tamp down the tension. She twisted her fingers and scooted forward.

Noah tugged her back by the coat. He gave her a slight smile. "We've got this."

"I know what's up there," she said. "What if Archimedes is watching?"

Noah turned to Zane, who studied his laptop. "You ID'd the street's security and traffic cameras?"

The computer expert nodded. "A couple of subjects have come into view based on the anemic descriptions of

Archimedes. None of them stayed. All of them met some-one and walked off. Archimedes is a loner. He's not here. Not in view." Zane adjusted his screen. "By the way, I hacked into the system. I have control of the cameras now."

Noah grinned. "Have I told you lately that I love you?"

"I never knew you cared." Zane tapped a few keys. "Still nothing. Reid's nowhere in sight."

Lyssa chewed on her lower lip. She had a bad feeling. She chanced a look at Noah.

His expression had grown solemn. Another scan of his phone. "Turn the cameras off, Zane. I don't want a record of Lyssa returning to that apartment. Not while the body is there."

Zane hit a few keystrokes. "Done."

"We can't wait for Reid any longer. Let's move out."

Elijah took point. He'd slipped his forensics case into a box and walked across the street as if he belonged. His entire demeanor had changed. Head bowed, he gave the impression of someone exhausted, going home from work, maybe who'd just been fired.

Noah placed his arm around Lyssa's shoulders and pulled her against his side. His warmth drove away the chill from the weather, but with each step across the side-walk, then into the street, she tensed against him. She had to stop; she needed to look around.

Her feet stopped moving. He pushed her forward, smil-ing down at her. "We're lovers," he whispered into her ear. "We're going home, and that old woman thinks we're eager to do the horizontal mambo. She's jealous."

He kissed the tip of her nose and led her toward the apartment building. "Relax. Almost there."

She tried. She wanted to sink into the heat of him, to forget everything and let him lead, but she couldn't. She couldn't allow herself to be vulnerable and unaware. If she'd been better prepared, better trained, she could have done something the night Archimedes attacked. Maybe Jack would still be alive. Maybe they would be a family, with a white picket fence, a baby and another on the way.

Ultra-aware of the movements around her, she caught sight of Rafe and Zane moving in opposite directions, then circling back. If she hadn't been watching for them, she would never have seen the tactic. These guys knew what they were doing.

Lyssa tried not to have too much hope, but a small fire ignited to life in her gut. Not big—she'd been singed before—but enough of a spark that she wondered if she might actually get out of this alive. She'd fully expected her confrontation with Archimedes to end with at least one of them dead, probably both.

As long as Archimedes couldn't hurt anyone else she loved, Lyssa could live with that. But now, maybe… She clung to Noah. He tightened his hold in return. She hadn't felt this way for a long, long time. Not since Archimedes had found her and forced her to make the toughest decision of her life.

Once they entered the apartment building, the subterfuge ceased. They headed straight up the stairs and down the empty hallway.

"Key?" Noah held out his hand. She gave it to him. He rotated the lock and pushed in the open door.

He stepped into the room, then stilled. Lyssa knew exactly what he saw. The memory of Gil's body and mutilated face had burned itself into her brain.

After several seconds he faced her, his expression completely calm except for a fury blazing in his eyes. Then the rage fled, replaced with a sympathy that made Lyssa's throat thicken as the emotions she'd fought to suppress resurfaced.

"You don't have to come in," he said, his deep voice soft and laced with compassion.

Part of her wanted to run, part of her always wanted to run, but she refused to give in. Archimedes had won too many battles. No longer.

"You might need me," she said, following him into the apartment.

"What a psycho," Elijah muttered, walking past her and kneeling next to the body.

"Search all the rooms," Noah ordered. "Look for anything out of place."

Zane and Rafe fanned out, beginning with the kitchen. Lyssa couldn't take her gaze away from Gil. Noah grabbed Lyssa's shoulders and turned her toward him. "Don't."

"I can handle it," she said, shrugging away from his grasp. "I have to."

She faced the room, forcing herself to study each shelf, each generic knickknack, each bit of decor she'd added to allay the landlord's suspicions she might have something to hide. There had to be a clue.

Nothing stood out.

"I don't notice—"

"Damn it," he whispered under his breath, gripping her arm and stepping back. He pulled out his phone and hit a couple of codes. "Zane," he called. "Get in here. Elijah, finish fast."

Lyssa froze at the urgency in his voice. What did he see?

Zane exited the bathroom and Noah tilted his head toward the living room. "We've got eyes. Check out the ivy."

Lyssa followed his gaze to the plant stand in the corner of her living room. A round electronic lens sat tucked on the edge of the pot.

"A camera?" she asked. Her body shivered. "Someone's watching? Now?"

"Move it, Rafe," Noah shouted. "We're on the clock."

Zane pulled out a palm-size screen. "Your jam is working. Audio *and* video." He studied the device, then hooked his handheld to one of the wires. Furiously he tapped his screen. "Come on, just a little longer."

His fingers quickened, but he started shaking his head. "I can't trace it. He has the signal bouncing all over the world." Finally Zane shoved the gadget into his pocket and disconnected the camera with a scowl. "He's good. Maybe I learned a few of his tricks."

"It better be more than a few," Noah said. "We can't afford to miss any opportunities. He knows we're onto him. If you know his ploys, he knows some of yours."

"You're sure it's Archimedes and not WitSec?" Lyssa asked, praying. She might be embarrassed that she'd run through the living room first thing in the morning with little more than a pair of panties on, but it was better than the alternative. Archimedes watching. "How long has it been there?"

"WitSec doesn't have the funds to set up this kind of toy." Zane knelt in front of the plant. "When's the last time you watered it?"

"Yesterday morning before work," she said.

"Then my guess is Archimedes set this up when he killed your handler. He had a lot of time in this apartment. He wanted to see you find the body. Bastard probably gets off watching you be afraid." Zane snagged the camera and slipped it into a plastic bag. "I'd like to turn the tables on him."

Noah's warm body stepped in close behind hers, pulling her against him. Despite her need to stay strong, Lyssa shivered at his nearness. She couldn't stop herself. She leaned into his comforting strength. She'd been fighting this battle alone for so very long. "He's sick."

"And obsessed."

Rafe came out of the bedroom. "The room's clean except for one anomaly. Lyssa, did you move your jewelry box recently?"

Lyssa placed her hand at her throat. "Yes."

"Then we're clear except the hall closet. Do you normally keep it locked?"

The question sent unease rolling through her. "I didn't even know it locked."

Noah's posture stiffened. "Stay with Rafe," he said softly.

Noah and Zane walked down the hall. Lyssa couldn't keep away. She had to know. Rafe's intense presence shadowed her. She peeked around the corner. Noah knelt down and in seconds sprang the knob free.

"He's the best," Rafe whispered. "Does that like he was born breaking and entering."

Noah opened the door.

A man's body tumbled into the hallway. She recognized the military cut, the square of his jaw. "Reid!"

Lyssa shoved forward and knelt beside Noah. The U.S. Marshal had been bound and gagged, his head bashed in, blood soaking his shirt.

Lyssa's hands placed her fingers on his wrist, searching, praying for a pulse. He looked too pale.

Noah tore off the duct tape. "Who did this, buddy?"

Reid's eyes flickered. "Warn…" was all he said before his head lolled to the side.

"Oh, God." Lyssa placed her hand over his chest. She could barely detect a heartbeat.

Noah leaned over and pressed two fingers against the man's carotid artery. "He needs an ambulance. Fast."

Zane tapped his earpiece. "Well, he's going to get help sooner than we expected. Someone called in an attack to this address. Cops are on their way."

Noah's expression turned to stone. "We've been set up. Out now."

Lyssa grabbed his arm, her fingers digging into him. "You aren't going to leave Reid, are you?"

She couldn't believe this. Jack had said Noah was loyal. She'd believed it. Had she been wrong about him?

He faced her. "Archimedes knows you have help. He knows we're here. If we get hauled down to police headquarters, he knows where to find you." Noah knelt by Reid, checking his pulse again. "An ambulance is coming. Elijah will make sure Reid makes it to the hospital, but *we* have to go." He looked at Elijah. "You get photos of the body?"

The forensics specialist nodded.

"Then we're out of here."

Zane peered out the window. "Black-and-whites. We're out of time."

"Take the fire escape," Noah ordered her.

Lyssa climbed onto the landing, his words finally sinking in. She paused. "Archimedes knows about you. Oh, God. What have I done?" She should never have called Reid. She should have done this alone. She was a fool.

Noah frowned at her. "Don't go shaky on me now, Lyssa. He would have known soon anyway. Hopefully it will irritate him enough he'll make a mistake."

"He hasn't yet, Noah." Lyssa took a deep breath, regret weighing heavy on her shoulders. "You're all in danger. I'm so sorry…"

Noah climbed a few steps down the ladder on the side of the building. "But we also learned that his obsession has escalated. He never left cameras before. He's getting desperate, and desperate men make mistakes. It's only a matter of time."

A matter of time before more people died. Lyssa didn't

know if she could live with any more of Archimedes's "messages."

She peered over the side of the building, down the rickety fire-escape ladder. Noah stared up at her, his stance confident, waiting for her, ready to catch her. She looked into his chocolate brown eyes.

Noah emitted certainty with every decision, every move, and Lyssa only knew one thing for sure. Now that Noah was in her life, he wouldn't willingly leave. Not as long as he breathed.

When she'd decided to confront Archimedes, she'd thought she'd be on her own—like always. Then Noah had come into her life. She'd been so determined she hadn't considered she'd be putting him and his team at risk.

What had she done?

THE FIFTY-INCH monitor flickered in the darkness. Archimedes sat forward in a leather chair in the pristine penthouse suite and watched the snow-filled screen.

"Alessandra, Alessandra," he said with a cluck of his tongue. "Haven't you learned?"

He typed in a few commands and the monitor cleared, but this time the room was empty. Except for his promise in blood.

They thought they could outsmart him. They might have disabled his signal and even taken one camera, but he never moved forward without a contingency plan. The second device worked perfectly.

Police flooded the room, then cordoned it off; they looked like little ants scurrying about on his screen. They'd be looking for Lyssa soon. WitSec would get involved. His little bird would sing to him all the information he needed.

As for Alessandra, he would have to be more clear with his message the next time.

He picked up a perfectly sharpened pencil and brand-new notepad from the walnut desk beside him. Switching signals, he rewound the tape, pausing the moment she'd entered the room.

She had been holding the hand of another man. A man who wanted her. Archimedes could see the desire in the intruder's eyes, in the way he infected Alessandra with his touch.

The pencil-tip broke.

He tossed the offending implement into the garbage can and took a second pencil. He stilled the tape.

"You belong to me," he whispered. "I am your destiny. We've waited ten years to be together. Nothing will stop us now."

A printer whirred and his rival's face stared back from the image it produced. "No one will stop us."

He walked to the closet and pulled out a new coat. He placed the bloodstained cashmere overcoat in the fireplace, sprinkled a small amount of accelerant and lit a match.

The fire exploded in warmth and the flames danced in celebration, consuming the evidence linking him to the waitress's unplanned death. Such a waste, but he refused to make a mistake. Not so close to having her.

Another lesson was in order.

Alessandra would be his.

And the man she leaned on—he would pay a heavy price for wanting her.

THE SMELLS AND sounds of Chicago's nightlife rang through the air: Italian spices, succulent barbecue, rumbling traffic, the clink of glasses, a few far-off sirens and laughter. Noah clutched Lyssa's resistant hand, anchoring her to his side. The city never turned completely dark, but that didn't mean peril didn't lurk in the shadows, no matter how inviting the music in the bars or how many people milled around enjoying the atmosphere.

Noah didn't want to think about how comfortable and right Lyssa's hand felt in his. To everyone watching, they seemed to be a couple walking the streets of Chicago at dinnertime. No one would guess they were on the look-out for a serial killer—a man whose face and identity remained a frustrating mystery.

A darkened alcove appeared just ahead. Noah slowed. The danger prowling just out of sight reminded him more of Afghanistan than a business district in one of America's largest cities. He scanned each potential vulnerability before he allowed Lyssa to move forward.

She wasn't any less vigilant. Her free hand hovered near her .45, poised for combat. He'd want her in his corner if he had to fight it out. He had no doubt she wouldn't give up in the midst of a battle. Which wouldn't be a problem as long as they were on the same page. If their plans of attack diverged, Noah could see fireworks in their future, and not the pleasurable kind.

Lyssa motioned left at the corner, and he swiftly circled to keep his body between the street and her. In front of a small mom-and-pop diner she stopped. He glanced at the hours posted on the glass. They'd be open a while longer, until 11:00 p.m.

"How often do you come here?" he asked.

"I stop by every few days or so for coffee. I try not to be predictable, and I pay cash," she added. "For everything."

"It's not realistic to go somewhere only once," he said, "even if it's ideal. You learned the game well."

"But not well enough." She didn't try to keep the bitterness from her voice. "You think he saw me here?"

"It's worth asking. We can't leave any possible lead untouched. Archimedes won't."

She fingered the chain at her throat. "I hate having a target on my back."

"I understand," Noah said. "Believe me." The last year or so overseas, chatter had started. The Falcon had become too well known. Some part of him relished the idea that his reputation alarmed the terrorists, but he knew if he was ever caught, if they ever discovered his identity, it would make the torture his friend Daniel Adams had survived look like amateur hour.

Noah had discovered intel that Daniel's abduction had partly come about because his enemies had put a price on the Falcon's head. Daniel was caught in the cross fire and ended up being captured in the process. One more person to whom Noah owed a debt. One more reason he should keep his activities secret from everyone.

He opened the door and Lyssa stepped inside. The scent of well-used fryers filtered through the room. The diner was like a thousand others with a pass-through window connecting the kitchen and dining room. A muscle-bound cook flipped a burger, dumped an order of fries and then slid a plate through to the shelf.

"Order up."

"Lyssa?" A woman with a freckled face smiled and walked over. "Usual table? Take a seat. I'll be right there."

"Usual table?" Noah raised an eyebrow.

"I should have stopped coming here," she said, grimacing. "Chastity has way too good a memory."

"Which might be to our advantage."

Noah escorted Lyssa into the small room and they took a seat. Chastity came over with a large smile. "How's it going? You're here late. Then again, so am I. They called me in. Your usual?" She tugged a worn order pad from her pocket.

Noah didn't need another moment to peg Chastity. She

wore her role with ease, knew the right thing to say. She'd obviously been a waitress a long time. Knew the game and was good at it. He bet she got good tips and could've worked anywhere, but he'd noticed the cook's attention linger on her a little too long as he'd handed over a plate. Not to mention her slight blush at the attention.

She worked here because of him.

"I'm not really hungry," Lyssa said. "How about a cup of hot tea?"

The woman turned to Noah. "And for you?"

Noah gave her a smile. "Coffee. And do I see home-made blueberry pie over there?"

She blushed. "Yes, sir. I baked it myself earlier."

He'd known. The blueberry stains under her nails gave her away. "Can't pass up blueberries," he said with a wink.

Chastity giggled and sent Lyssa a grin. "He's a keeper."

She left them alone. Lyssa leaned across the table. "What are you doing?" she whispered through clenched teeth. "Are you *trying* to grab Archimedes's attention? You're being memorable. I thought being invisible was the first rule."

"Chastity will remember more easily if she's not suspicious," Noah said. "Besides, we're not following the rules any longer. Relax. You're making *me* tense."

"I should have seen it. You *want* to make Archimedes angry," she hissed. "I'm bait for a man who's killed dozens of people. I have the right to be tense. Especially when you don't tell me we're going with *my* plan."

She glared at Noah, daring him to deny it.

He couldn't. He doubted their visit here would result in a hit, but maybe Chastity could provide information. "Your plan, with adjustments. Rafe's watching." Noah tilted his head toward the window.

Lyssa glanced outside. The operative stood near the

bus stop, his eye patch and beard visible when he lifted his head in acknowledgment. Moments later, he returned to perusing the paper.

"I didn't notice him tailing us. I thought he was observing the cops."

"He was. He switched off with Zane. Someone will always be watching, Lyssa. Our job is to never let you out of sight."

Her leg bounced under the booth's table. "He's in plain sight. It's a mistake. Everyone I've involved is now dead or in the hospital."

"It's our job, Lyssa. We do it well."

She let out a long sigh. "Okay, then what do we do now?"

"Talk to Chastity, maybe luck into a description that will fit with some of the other sightings. Zane is reviewing Archimedes's records. With Reid still unconscious, he had to force his way into the system. Elijah tried to tone down his smarts so he could make friends with the local CSIs. He's checking out the crime scene information."

Her lists twisted. "You won't find anything. Trust me. My plan was easier. I sit in my apartment and wait for him. Let him come to me. Simple. Straightforward."

"It gives him all the power—and the advantage. That's the last thing I want to do." Noah leaned forward. "Give me a few days to fine-tune an approach. For Jack."

"You'll use anything to get me to fall in line, won't you?" Lyssa toyed with the necklace around her throat.

What was on the end of it escaped from beneath her collar. Noah recognized it. Jack's engagement ring. The sight of the diamond twisted Noah's gut. The memory haunted him in a different way from Lyssa. "You must miss him."

"He shouldn't have died that way." Lyssa rubbed her ring finger, obviously trying to tamp down the memories.

"Archimedes just shot Jack in the head." She shivered. "He died for me."

Noah placed his hand on hers and squeezed. "Always the hero."

Lyssa swiped at a tear. "Yeah."

"I miss him, too." Noah swallowed down the regret. His friend had deserved to be happy. So had Lyssa. "Jack saved my life. And Reid's. We were on special assignment. The whole thing went south. Jack was always the best shot. He came back for me and took out the sniper. He was a good man. I'd be dead without him."

He met her emerald gaze. Something they had in common.

With a last push of the memories aside, Noah shifted in his seat. The past was over. He had a very dangerous present to deal with. "We'll get Archimedes, Lyssa. I won't stop until you don't have to run. I left you once. I won't do it again."

Chastity walked over to their table with their order on her tray. Noah looked up at her with a smile, then he frowned. Perspiration dotted her forehead. Her skin had gone gray.

"Are you okay?"

She swayed then collapsed at his feet.

Noah vaulted from his seat and knelt beside her. Her muscles had gone rigid. She met his gaze, her eyes wide with fear. She tried to speak, but couldn't move. He sniffed her breath. No odor, but it had to be poison.

Her chest rose once, twice, then simply stopped.

"No!" Lyssa cried out.

He started CPR even though he knew she had no chance.

The cook dashed around the counter. "Chastity!"

A customer dialed for an ambulance.

Noah knew there was no hope, but he didn't stop. He met Lyssa's gaze and shook his head slowly.

She closed her eyes and stared down at her feet.

Then her lids widened. He followed her line of sight.

Chastity's order book had opened.

On the very last page. Infinity.

Archimedes's signature.

Just below the infinity he'd included a new, second symbol. A small spiral moving counterclockwise on the page, followed by two words.

I'm waiting.

Chapter Four

Lyssa sank to her knees and clutched Chastity's hand. "No. Don't let him do this."

Praying it wasn't true, Lyssa bowed her head. She could barely breathe. "Fight, Chastity. Fight him."

The entire diner froze in shock.

Noah kept up the CPR for what seemed like forever. He paused and held his finger to her carotid. "I'm sorry," he said, looking up at the cook, who hovered to Noah's left. "She's gone."

"Oh, God, Chastity. You can't be dead." The cook's pained voice pierced the crowd.

The waitress's eyes stared wide at the ceiling, unseeing. With a grimace, Noah forced her eyes closed.

The diner erupted into chaos. A waitress screamed. A wave of panic hurled through the restaurant. Half the patrons ran out the front.

Lyssa gripped Chastity's hand even tighter then squeezed her eyes tight. "This can't be happening." Chastity had done nothing to deserve this. She was a nice waitress who was good at her job, never hurt anyone.

"Why?" Lyssa looked up at Noah. "Why did he have to kill her?"

Noah didn't answer, but then again, Lyssa didn't expect one. What answer could there be?

"Damn him," she said.

"Rafe, you see anything?" Noah hissed into the nearly invisible communication device.

The response couldn't be good. The muscle in his jawline throbbed. "Meet us around back. We're getting out of here."

Noah leaned over and with two fingers picked up Chastity's order book by the corner.

"What are you doing?" Lyssa said under her breath. "That's evidence."

"It won't do the cops any good. And it's our only clue." He grabbed her hand and pulled her to her feet. "Let's go."

Lyssa's teeth ground together, but he was right. God, she hated leaving Chastity, but the woman was gone. One more person she'd placed in Archimedes's path. One more reason she had to stop the serial killer.

She grabbed her purse and let Noah tug her through the few morbidly curious customers who lingered in the diner. She shoved into the kitchen. His gaze swept the room and she headed to the back door.

"We clear?" Rafe said into his microphone.

The cook ran into the kitchen, his cheeks wet with tears. "You're not going anywhere," he growled. "What did you do to my Chastity?"

He lunged at Noah. In a blur of moves Noah had the big man on his back, his forearm to the guy's throat.

"We didn't hurt her," Noah said, his voice low and deadly. "Now, when she picked up that last order, did she do anything different than normal? Was anyone else back here?"

Lyssa shoved her hand into her coat to grip her weapon. "Is he here?" Her half panicked, half vengeful gaze searched the kitchen then through the pass-through window at the few people left in the diner.

"This was a message not an attack." Noah pressed his arm harder against the guy's neck. "Answer the question. Who else was back here?"

The man struggled against Noah but couldn't escape the tight grip. Finally, the cook stilled and scowled up at his captor. "Why do you care? You're running away. At least my other waitress, Sally, was willing to watch over Chastity, keep those vultures away. Only a coward would hide. Or the guilty."

Noah lifted his arm and backed away. The cook sat up, holding his throat. Lyssa knelt next to him, taking in the man's grief-stricken eyes. "I know how you feel," she said, her voice strained. "We know who did this. He killed my fiancé. Please, help us."

The man's shoulders sagged, his big heart obviously broken. Another tear slid down his cheek. "She was excited. Some guy left her an envelope. He told her he'd stiffed her on a tip. She didn't remember that happening, but it was three twenties." The cook's brow furrowed. "She remembers—" he swallowed "—remembered *every* customer. Who did this?"

Noah held out his hand to the man and helped him to his feet. "Archimedes."

"The serial killer?" The cook's mouth gaped open. "I saw a news report about him. They called him a ghost."

"Did you see Chastity talk to him?"

"The guy met her out back. No one saw him but Chastity." The big man rubbed his bald head. "Oh, babe."

"Where's the envelope Archimedes gave her?" Noah asked.

"She put it in her locker."

"Get in here, Rafe," Noah growled into the communication device.

Within seconds Rafe shoved through the back door, slamming it open, gun raised.

"There's an envelope in one of the lockers. The victim was poisoned, so be careful. Take one of the bills. Leave the others for the cops." He nodded at Chastity's order book, which had slid across the floor when he'd taken down Al. "Bag that, too. I want to know what he used. It acted fast."

Rafe tugged a blue glove from inside his vest and headed through the door the cook pointed out.

Noah crossed his arms. "Listen to me carefully, Al." The cook's eyes widened. "Your name tag," Noah pointed out. "Archimedes is after this woman." He indicated Lyssa. "He's killed a lot of people. We could use your help."

"I couldn't even protect Chastity." Al looked as if he might collapse again. "Maybe the cops can help."

"The feds can't catch him, the cops can't catch him. I will."

Sirens sounded in the distance. The look on Noah's face sent a chill through Lyssa.

"They're coming. I need some cover, Al. If we get pulled into custody, she's a sitting duck for this psycho."

Al's expression changed and he shoved up his shirt-sleeve. He had a tattoo that read *Semper fidelis.* Always faithful.

"You get this guy, make him pay for what he did to Chastity and the cops don't hear nothing from me except that envelope."

Noah gave the man a sharp nod. "You got it, Marine."

Rafe slipped back into the room, a baggie in his hand with a twenty-dollar bill showing. "There was a pin in the envelope. Pricked her skin. Not much here. My guess is batrachotoxin because of the amount."

"Poison-dart frog? You're kidding," Noah said, turning

to Al. "Tell the cops to be careful. My friend here has some strange hobbies. Knows his stuff. Something the size of a few grains of table salt will kill."

Al's face paled and he nodded.

Lyssa took his hands in hers and squeezed them. She met his gaze, regret nearly strangling her. "I'm so very, very sorry. She was a kind person."

"Wish I'd told her how I felt," he said, his voice barely a whisper. "I'd known her for years. She was too good for me...could have worked anywhere, but she stayed. Maybe I shouldn't have even smiled at her. Then she'd have left. She'd still be alive."

Lyssa could relate. Her life the past two years was a one big regret. Chastity was just the latest.

He tugged his hands away from her before wiping his face with his apron.

Lyssa looked over at Noah, his stance guarded, his eyes shifting toward the door Rafe had disappeared through. Had she done the same thing? Allowed him into her chaos only to put his life in danger? Her phone call to Reid had caused nothing but trouble. She had a feeling it would get worse.

Two police cars skidded to a halt in front of the diner. Shouts sounded from outside.

"We've got to go," Noah said to Lyssa, pulling his gun from the holster and heading to the back door of the diner.

Al pushed it open, and Noah rushed Lyssa through the exit and into the alley behind the restaurant. Rafe followed and slammed the door behind them.

"Stay back while Rafe checks the car."

In short order, Rafe maneuvered around, then under the vehicle, a device in his hand. He'd obviously done this before. "Clear." He jumped into the driver's side and started the car, then nodded at Noah.

"Go!" he shouted at Lyssa. "In the car."

She raced across the alley and into the SUV. Noah followed. "Get out of here, Rafe!"

The vehicle peeled out the side street, just in time to see two more police cars and an ambulance speed into view.

"No matter what Al says, the customers will remember us," Lyssa said, looking back at the commotion surrounding the diner.

"It can't be helped. Besides, we're not staying in Chicago. I'm getting you to safety. In Texas." He turned on Rafe. "You didn't see *anything?*"

"Not a damn thing, Noah."

Rafe turned a corner, the diner faded away, just like the past year of Lyssa's life. Her fingernails dug into her palms. She had to *do* something. Chastity's death was her fault. "Can I look at the book?" she asked.

Noah handed her a sealed bag. She viewed the order pad, still open to Archimedes's note, through the clear plastic.

She stared at the spiral symbol and the message. "What is he trying to tell me?" she asked. "What does this mean?"

One glance from Noah sent a shiver through her. His expression had hardened, his eyes had gone flint cold.

"He's communicating, all right. He wants you to know he'll find you. Wherever you go."

EVEN INSIDE THE SUV, frozen ice laced the air. The headlights illuminated the road leading to the small airport, the asphalt shimmering with ice crystals. Noah gripped the steering wheel, his knuckles white as he squeezed the frustration into submission. He should've dragged Lyssa to his plane the moment he'd arrived in Chicago.

He didn't delude himself with the hope that the outcome at the diner could have been different. He doubted leaving town would've saved Chastity. Archimedes had planted his message carefully, wanting Lyssa to know he'd been watching.

The psycho was toying with her, and Noah had fallen into the plans. He hated making a mistake; he wouldn't underestimate Archimedes again. He'd allowed Lyssa's arguments in that alley to sway him. No more.

He glanced into the rearview mirror, studying her expression. A woman had died in front of her, but Lyssa hadn't broken down. Still, he could see the unease settling over her. Archimedes had peeled away her confidence in Noah and his team.

He had to regain her trust. Once she was at the safe house in Dallas, they'd all regroup and he'd figure out a way to corner Archimedes without putting Lyssa in danger.

Noah turned the vehicle toward Koritz Field, the lights on the single runway in view.

Rafe leaned forward in his seat. "You landed the Lear here? Cutting it a little close, weren't you, Noah?"

"I like to keep the enemy guessing." He lifted a brow at the former Green Beret who Noah trusted more than anyone to have his back.

Rafe simply shook his head. "You're insane."

Lyssa peered out the front window. "What's the problem?"

"The runway is too short, especially at night," Rafe said. "Barely able to handle Noah's new plane. He took a risk landing here."

"The field is uncontrolled. No air traffic control tower."

"Which makes sneaking in and out easier," Lyssa said, admiration lacing her voice. She leaned forward, her arms resting on the back of the seat. "Archimedes can't follow the plane. That's good."

Noah grinned at her. "I'm glad someone appreciates my brilliant strategy."

"Smart doesn't necessarily equate with sane." Rafe scowled at him, adjusting his eye patch.

"You never have liked to fly."

"With you," Rafe snapped.

Lyssa said nothing. Not a smile at the forced joking. He met Rafe's gaze and the man shrugged. He'd tried—he'd also been halfway serious.

Her silence sent the hairs on the back of Noah's neck to attention. He didn't like the contemplative look on her face. He'd seen it before—on Ransom Grainger's face when his boss was planning a mission.

He pulled the SUV into the parking lot next to the only other car at this time of night. Probably belonging to the fixed-based operator's lineman. Another reason Noah had chosen this little FBO. At this time of year, there was no skydiving and therefore, the airport was pretty much barren, especially so close to midnight. He favored two types of setups. Either one with too many people or hardly anyone. Both had advantages and disadvantages.

When it came to Archimedes, deserted won the battle. The guy could blend into a crowd. Which is why not one identifiable description existed of the man who had killed so many people.

Noah slid from the seat. "Wait here. I'll make sure we're fueled so we can take off."

"No need," Rafe said from the passenger side.

"The Lear's ready? Who?"

"Zane. Our favorite computer jockey evidently likes propellers as much as you do. Elijah's staying behind to analyze the evidence with the other forensics squints and hopefully get us a lead. He'll join us as soon as he can."

Lyssa twisted her fingers in her lap. "I think Elijah should go with you. Now."

Her voice was too calm. Noah twisted in his seat, that bad feeling settling in the pit of his stomach. "You mean go with *us*."

"No," Lyssa said. "I'm not leaving with you. Two people are dead—and Reid could die—all because of me. I have to *do* something, and I'm not involving anyone else." She opened her hand. "Give me the keys to the SUV, Noah. Archimedes won't follow you. You'll be safe, but I'm staying. When this is over, I'll leave the car for you. I'm sure you can find it."

He gripped the keys in his hand. "Hell, no. You're not remaining in Chicago while that guy's still on the loose."

"I made a mistake. I shouldn't have called Reid." She met his gaze with an unwavering one of her own. "I'm doing what I should have done in the first place. I'm going to my apartment and wait with my 12-gauge across my lap and my .45 at my side. He won't get away again."

"You try this alone, and he'll change it up. He'll attack from behind or poison the air, or God knows what," Noah argued. "*We* need to flank him." He slammed out of the SUV's front seat and scooted in the back beside her. "We've just gotten started. Give us a chance, Lyssa."

"You're not going to stuff me in some fortress in the middle of Texas. I can see it on your face, Noah. You want to hide me away. Tell me I'm wrong."

"The idea has merit," he said but retreated the moment she glared at him. "Look, we need to regroup. We'll be analyzing every minuscule piece of information that's been collected about Archimedes. We're going to uncover the connection, and we're going to find a way to trap him."

"I gave you two chances. Reid's in the hospital. Chastity is dead. Go back to Texas."

Noah gritted his teeth. "Rafe, finish the preflight for me."

His friend said nothing. He exited the vehicle and walked out to the plane. Noah gripped her shoulders. "I'm not letting you do this."

"You can't stop me." She turned her palm up. "Keys."

He shoved them into his front pocket. She followed the movement with her eyes. The challenge in them scared the hell out of him.

"There's only one way for this to end," she said softly. "He wants me. I'm going to give him what he wants. Hand me the keys."

"I'm not going to convince you to come with us, am I?"

She shook her head. "You did what you could. Tell Reid…if he wakes up, tell him I appreciate what he tried to do. And that I'm sorry."

"Damn you, Lyssa. You're going out there to die, aren't you?"

"I'm not planning on it." She straightened her back, her chin lifted in determination. "But he's going to die, Noah. And if I die, too, I'll have done the right thing. For everyone."

"I'm not letting that happen." Before she could say another word, Noah grabbed her by the waist and tugged her out of the SUV so fast she didn't fight him.

He'd obviously taken her by surprise. Good.

He heaved her up over his shoulder and placed the keys on the driver-side front tire.

The calm lasted for a second or two. She twisted against him, squirming. "What do you think you're doing?"

"Saving your life," Noah said with a grunt when she kneed him in the gut. "Stop it or I'll drop you."

She didn't obey.

Fighting against the she-cat in his arms, pretty sure

she'd bruised some ribs, he climbed up the plane's steps. Zane's mouth fell open but he moved aside.

"Let me down, Noah," Lyssa bit out, "or I'll call the cops."

He dumped her into a seat and clicked the seat belt around her. She unlatched it and sprang to her feet. She shoved her hands at his chest, then heaved her body weight at him, shoulder first. He stumbled back and gripped her arms. "Lyssa, calm down. I'm not leaving you. You're not in this fight alone, do you hear me? You. Are. Not. Alone."

She shook her head back and forth. "Don't you get it? You could die. You could all *die!* And it would be *my* fault. Again. I won't let that happen. I *can't*.

"I can't," she whispered over and over again.

Her fists gripped his shirt hard and he hugged her against him, tight. She tried to push him away, she fought against him, but he wouldn't let her. Not now. He strengthened his hold, waiting for her struggling to stop. The torment in each movement and groan stripped his heart. He didn't know how long it took, but finally, her body sagged in exhaustion, her breathing ragged.

With her energy gone, he cradled her in his arms and sat down in one of the leather seats. He ran his hand along her hair. He met Rafe's gaze over her.

Take off? he mouthed, knowing his friend could do it, also knowing he hated to pilot the plane.

Rafe gave him a curt nod, then motioned to Zane.

They disappeared into the cockpit.

Noah shifted her off of him, and she let him rebuckle her seat belt.

"You shouldn't do this," she said to him, her voice flat, her face haunted. "You know how many lives he's ruined. He'll ruin yours. I know he will. It'll be my fault."

The plane lifted off. He'd never have known the runway

was too short. Rafe had quite the touch. Noah took in Lyssa's nearly ghostlike complexion. He tugged her hands between his. Her fingers were ice-cold and he rubbed them, warming the frigid skin. "It's not your fault. It's his. He made the choice."

She wouldn't look at him but stared down at her hands. "Did you see Al's face? He loved Chastity. And because I chose to go into that diner one day, because I couldn't resist a friendly smile some days…" A shiver ran through her, she ripped her hands away from him, clenching her fists, her knuckles white. "I hate him. I hate what he's done." She lifted her tortured gaze to his. "I hate that you're next."

"We'll be ready for him," Noah promised, praying he could keep his word. If he didn't, Lyssa wouldn't survive. And if she didn't, neither would he.

The hum of the plane's engine quieted as they reached a cruising altitude.

"You can't guarantee…" She pressed the heels of her hands to her eyes. "You don't know…" Her eyes glazed over and she stared out the window into the darkness that cocooned the aircraft. "Life couldn't have been better that day. The day that changed my world forever. I'd fallen in love with Jack. We'd moved in together. At work, I'd just been tapped to do a high-profile press conference translating for the Russian president. Everything was perfect…"

She crossed her hands over her stomach, the agony almost too difficult to watch. Jack had been a lucky man. To have a woman's love like that, Noah could only imagine.

"Archimedes destroyed everything. When I walked in the house that night, he'd been aiming the gun at Jack. He swung around. Jack yelled at me to run then rushed Archimedes, placing himself between me and that madman. The guy just shot Jack in cold blood, in the head, then he turned to me…" Her voice broke. "I could see Archimedes smile, his mouth visible through the hole in the ski mask he wore. He held out his hand to me. 'Come,' he said. I ran."

Noah had never heard her version of that night. He wanted to drag her into his arms, out of the nightmare, but she'd locked herself in the past.

"Lyssa," he said, his voice soft.

Her eyes snapped open.

"Did he ever point the gun at you?"

"Of course he did. Jack jumped in front of it."

"That's not what you said. You said Archimedes swung around when you came in the room."

Her forehead furrowed. "I guess…what are you getting at?"

"I think there's a reason you're still alive. Archimedes doesn't want you dead. He *wants* you. We can use that to our advantage. If you'll let us.

Noah gripped her hand. "He's dropping a twisted trail of bread crumbs, and you're the prize he's waiting for."

CANDLELIGHT FLICKERED AT the small corner table of the Italian restaurant, illuminating the face of the woman across from Archimedes. The fragrant spices of the exclusive D.C. eatery danced on the air.

There was no name over the doorway—just another reason he frequented the place. Enough cash bought a table… and discretion.

His companion was attractive enough, unassuming. Her eyelashes fluttered and she gazed at him, something akin to adoration.

She wasn't Alessandra, of course. Alessandra was perfection.

He lifted the glass of red wine, letting the berries, vanilla, mocha and oak aroma tease his palate. "To our three-month anniversary." He smiled at her. "You, Rose Wright, have placed my greatest desire within reach."

Her cheeks flushed and she bit her lip, taking a dainty sip of the Petrus as he, too, gifted his taste buds with the fifteen-hundred-dollar-a-bottle wine to celebrate his Chicago success. While the police and the feds scurried like rats, he waited, waited for Alessandra to prove her worth.

"I've never met anyone like you." Rose sighed.

The waiter approached and placed their plates of pasta in front of them.

Archimedes frowned, staring at his dish. Spots. He could see the spots. The side of his head began to throb and he pressed the heel of his hand against his temple.

"Take them back," he snapped. "We want *clean* china."

The waiter scowled and snatched the dinners. "Whatever."

Rose squirmed in her chair, her face going pale. He touched her cheek, forcing himself not to wince as his bare finger came into contact with her germ-infested skin.

"Nothing but the best for you, my dearest Rose."

The waiter soon returned. "I—I'm very sorry, sir. I didn't realize who you were." He practically bowed leaving them alone, perfectly pristine plates sitting in front of them.

Rose smiled in awe. "How do they—?"

"I have a variety of interests, my dear. The owner once assisted me and I helped him gain financing to open up the restaurant. Clearly, the waiter is new. He won't make the same mistake again."

Archimedes studied the unspoiled fork and sampled the pasta. Perfect, as always. "How is work, my dear?"

Rose frowned and leaned forward. "Terrible," she said, her voice barely a whisper. "My boss was almost killed yesterday."

"Almost?"

The man should be dead. Archimedes had killed more than one with a blow with exactly that force and position… except, Reid Nichols had fought longer than most against the paralytic drug. He'd moved slightly, impacting the trajectory and pressure. Interesting. Just the slightest change had spared the man's life.

Luckily, the marshal's survival wouldn't alter Archimedes's plans. His disguise would misdirect any inquiries.

"He's still alive, but he's in a coma. They've clamped down tight on security." She lowered her voice. "They think a serial killer did it. That woman I told you about last week, the one who is the only witness, she's on the run now. They can't find her."

"Really?"

He let the slight hint of red chili in the sauce tingle in his mouth and hid a smile of satisfaction. He knew exactly what had happened to Alessandra. And *who*.

Archimedes had thought he'd recognized the man at her side. A bit of research on the plane from Chicago had verified his rival's identity.

Noah Bradford. Supposed electronics wunderkind. Wealthy, and his company's contracts with Homeland Security and the Department of Defense were the envy of many a high school geek who wanted to make it big.

There was Gates, Jobs and Bradford.

This time, though, Bradford had no idea who he was dealing with.

The question was, why would someone like Bradford step out of his pristine corporate CEO position and partner up with three unidentifiable men? Why would Bradford care about Alessandra? Archimedes would have to dig deeper. There had to be a connection.

Not that it mattered.

He slipped his phone from the pocket of his fine cashmere coat and opened the map. After zooming out a few times, a small dot blinked.

So, his prey had gone to Texas.

He looked up from the screen to his companion. She spun her fork in the spaghetti and stuffed it in her mouth. Sauce marred her chin. He sighed.

No, she definitely wasn't Alessandra.

"I'm afraid we have to cut tonight short, my dear." He indicated his phone. "Business call. I have another plane to catch."

She bowed her head, clearly disappointed. "But you just got back. I'd hoped we could spend the night…together."

He struggled to hide the shudder of revulsion. At least he had an excuse. "My job shouldn't take long, and then I'll be able to show you how I really feel."

He folded the napkin perfectly eight times and grimaced at the mess she'd dropped on the plate. Lipstick stains and marinara sauce smudged the white linens.

Disgusting.

Even if he'd desired her, she would require too much work to perfect.

She wasn't Alessandra.

No one was.

A small plane ride and his message would be delivered.

Noah Bradford would soon understand.

Alessandra would receive the next clue…her next test.

They couldn't hide from him.

He was too smart, too clever.

Archimedes stood, waiting for Rose. She stumbled to her feet and he escorted her out of the restaurant to the Metro. At just after midnight, the train still bustled. A man in a suit shoved them aside in his hurry to board the red line.

The pain in Archimedes's head throbbed. He scowled and pressed against the sharp agony.

Rose clutched his hand, digging her fingernails into his palm, an act she'd pay for. "That man d-doesn't matter."

Archimedes tugged her onto the train and sat across from the insolent passenger who focused on his tablet computer.

A few quick strokes and Archimedes had exactly what he needed. He led Rose off the train.

"Where are we going?" she asked. "This isn't our stop."

He ignored her. He tapped an image.

The red-line train pulled away. Through the window, Archimedes could see the man convulse as an overload of electrical current pulsed through his fingertips from the tablet. He fell to the floor.

Dead. Heart stopped.

Another lesson learned. They *would* respect him.

Sooner or later, *everyone* would understand.

Chapter Five

The dim light of dawn brushed the edge of the horizon by the time Noah ordered Rafe to head directly to the safe house. At least the Texas weather cut them a break. Ten degrees warmer made for a big difference, even in the dead of winter.

From the backseat of the rented SUV that CTC had supplied, Noah scanned the area surrounding the new location. A screened-in front porch encased the ranch-style house. One more barrier. He liked the setup.

"Drive past it and circle around," he ordered Rafe, even though they'd serpentined through the Dallas–Fort Worth area for the past ninety minutes.

On high alert, his hand on his weapon, Zane peered out the other side of the vehicle. Normally, Noah would have taken the front passenger seat, but he'd slipped into the back with Lyssa.

Surprising how her new name fell off his tongue so easily. He'd almost stopped thinking of her as Alessandra. He glanced over at her. She'd fallen into a deep sleep on the plane. Nearly thirty-six hours awake had scraped her nerves raw. The nap had returned some color to her cheeks. That, along with a hint of embarrassment and a flash of resentment in her eyes.

He'd half expected her to hightail it when they'd landed.

He'd practically kidnapped her, after all. She'd been quiet since they'd landed. He had to wonder what she plotted behind those compelling green eyes. She gripped her duffel tight. The shotgun was just inside. He didn't blame her for keeping the weapon close, as long as she didn't use it on him.

He'd told her the truth. Maybe the sleep had made her see sense. She was smart. She'd stayed alive for two years. They *all* needed to regroup. He didn't like being in retreat, but better alive and together than the alternative.

Right now, Archimedes had the advantage.

Noah didn't anticipate the situation to last long.

"Appears clear," Rafe said, taking another turn around the block in the suburb north of Fort Worth.

"Agree," Zane added.

"Go inside," Noah ordered. "Check it out."

The SUV pulled up to the house. Zane jumped out and keyed in the code to the garage door. The metal slid up, strangely quiet.

Lyssa slipped her hand beneath her coat. Noah didn't say a word.

A few minutes later, Zane motioned them forward. Rafe pulled the car into the garage, but Noah didn't breathe until they were sealed inside the house.

Lyssa finally removed her hand from her .45. "You've got me here. Now what?"

Her gaze dared Noah. He knew very well he didn't have much time. Lyssa was resourceful; she'd find her way back to Chicago if that's what she really wanted.

"Now we locate Archimedes." Noah punched in a code in the garage. "I've scrambled the garage-door signal. If anyone was watching, they won't be getting in. He walked directly into the small dining room. "Set up here."

Zane nodded, tugging his laptop from its case. "I need secure internet."

Noah glanced over at Lyssa. He could almost feel the nerves shooting through her body. "Want to go out back? I have to hook up a satellite system."

She gave a sharp nod and followed him onto the porch then into the yard. There was a chill in the air, but not so much that he needed gloves. He positioned the small dish so that it faced the sky and flipped open a case from inside his jacket.

He twisted a few screws and lifted the weather cover. "How are you feeling?"

She scuffed the grass with her shoe. "Embarrassed. Rafe and Zane must think I'm certifiable."

"Nah. They know you're exhausted and that you've been through hell." Squatting down, he secured the equipment before pulling out his phone to position the receiver.

Lyssa said nothing. She crossed her arms over her jacket then slipped her hand inside, as if reassuring herself that protection was near. Noah observed her carefully. Even while she spoke, she scanned the backyard, searching for anything out of place. Noah had been in life-threatening situations more often than not since he'd joined the Marines, but there was always an end to the mission. How would it be, month after month, year after year, to never let your guard down?

Walking the twelve-foot concrete wall encasing the rear perimeter of the house, she reached the gate and yanked. It didn't budge; it was secured shut with a series of large steel bolts.

Finalizing the satellite positioning, he strode to the screen door and cracked it open. "Check out the connection, Zane. We'll be a few more minutes."

He studied Lyssa across the yard. She stiffened, her expression one of caution.

"Are you planning to run?" he asked.

She didn't respond but returned to the gate and tugged at it again. "If he finds us, how do I escape? I'm trapped here."

Noah joined her. Without hesitation, he flicked open a panel painted to look like concrete. "The code is seven-nine-one-three." He pressed the numbers. The bolts slid back.

With an easy push, Lyssa swung the heavy gate open and peered into a small carport behind the yard. An escape vehicle waited.

"Gassed and ready to go." Noah resecured the backyard. "The keys are in a similar hiding place on the backside of the wall. Satisfied?"

Her incredulous expression, then quick nod made his lips quirk. Her body seemed to relax a bit.

"Are you going to use the code and car to leave?"

With a sigh, she rubbed the back of her neck. "I may have lost it on the plane, but what I said was true. You're in danger. It would be better if you and your friends let me finish this on my own."

She gazed up at the cloudy sky. "I want it over."

He could see the emotion welling in her eyes. She'd used up all her reserves.

"I want you safe, Lyssa. You're not a prisoner, even though part of me would like to lock you up at the North Pole until this psycho is out of your life." Noah rubbed his hands up and down her arms. "We're hundreds of miles away from Archimedes. You've been battling him solo for too long, Lyssa. Lean on me...on us. We can help."

She blinked several times in quick succession. "I've been

alone a long time, Noah. I can't promise anything. I don't know how to trust anymore. That ability died with Jack."

Turning away, she walked back to the house. He cursed himself for listening to Reid and abandoning her to the system back then. When Archimedes had found her in hiding shortly after being placed in WitSec, Noah had hoped he was doing the right thing. What if somehow the killer had broken into Noah's systems, using him to track Alessandra. He couldn't chance it.

He'd been wrong. He refused to let her go. Not again. She wouldn't get rid of him, no matter what she said or did.

He scanned the periphery then followed her inside, locking the doors and setting the external alarm.

Lyssa hovered near the dining room table. "What are those?" she asked, staring at the six-inch-tall group of files at one end.

"The information from WitSec connecting to Archimedes," Zane answered.

"I thought there'd be more," Noah said. "Are you sure this is everything?"

Rafe pulled up a chair. "Zane and I agree this can't be it. Some of the files must be missing."

"Zane, can you bore into Justice through a back door?" Noah asked, thumbing through the documents. "Take another look?"

"Probably." Zane looked up from his keyboard. "I'm not just crossing the legal line on this, Noah, I'm jumping with both feet into big trouble if we're caught."

"And your point is?"

Zane grinned. "Thought you should know why we'll end up in jail if we're caught."

"No choice," Noah said. "With Reid in the hospital, I don't know who to trust. Just don't leave a trail. I hate being locked up."

"Who do you think you're talking to?" Zane asked. "My zeros and ones are invisible." He lowered his head and tapped away at the keyboard.

Biting her lip in concentration, Lyssa thumbed through the files, taking time to read each name. "There are names I don't see here." She looked up. "Archimedes got to someone at WitSec, didn't he?"

"That's what Reid believes," Noah said. "It's probably how Archimedes found you."

Lyssa settled into a mahogany chair at one end and pulled off a small stack of files.

"Chastity's information isn't here, of course." Rafe patted the remaining stack. "And while we were on the plane I caught word of another strange death. A woman set on fire only a few blocks from the diner where Chastity died."

"Archimedes likes fire," Lyssa said, her voice matter-of-fact.

That flat note captured Noah's attention. Ever since she'd entered the house, she'd encased herself in an iron curtain, maintaining precarious control. He understood the necessity, but she was on the edge. Her fingers shook just a bit, and yet she powered through.

She awed him.

"Thirty percent of his crimes involve either death or destruction by fire," she added. "The arson investigators haven't been able to identify the accelerant that he uses. All they know is that it burns fast and hot and completely disintegrates most of the evidence."

Zane's hands paused on the keyboard, his expression stunned. "How—?"

"The fact leaked out after a warehouse fire killed the owner of a freight company. It surprises you I want to know exactly what he's doing? And where he is all the time?" Lyssa stared at him, unblinking. "Why would I give him the upper hand?"

"Will you marry me?" Zane blurted out. "I love a smart woman with guts."

"Just keep your eyes on your keyboard." Noah planted himself between Zane and Lyssa.

Zane gave Noah a jaunty salute and huddled back on the computer, but not without a smirk on his face.

Okay, so Noah hadn't hidden the fact that he liked Lyssa. A lot. He glanced over at her, too hesitant for his own peace of mind.

He'd expected her to be looking at him, expected that shot of awareness that tingled just below the surface of the skin to bounce between them, but she'd turned him off.

Instead, she took a folder from the shorter stack in front of her.

Noah placed his hand on hers. "You don't want to—"

Lyssa opened the file anyway. She let out a shocked gasp. "I can't even tell if this is a man or a woman. What did Archimedes do?"

Noah tugged the file away from her, but not before he caught a glance of an autopsy photo of a corpse with a bloated face floating at the edge of a slow-moving river. "One thing about Archimedes, I'm sure you know, is that his M.O.s are all over the place. He's an encyclopedia of modus operandi."

"I know. I've been researching him for two years," Lyssa opened another file. "Newspapers don't print these kinds of photos, but I know there are victims from all over the country. Mostly on the East and West coasts. Men and women, old and young, professional and homeless. I can't find a connection."

"That's why the feds have no case and no clue," Noah said. "Except you. You've heard his voice."

"A whisper two years ago. Even I know it's not enough."

Noah knelt in front of her chair. "There *is* a connection. We just haven't found it yet."

"Lyssa." He waited until his patience forced her to meet his gaze. Her dead eyes terrified him. He gripped her hands. "I'm telling you right now, we'll find the connection. We'll find him."

She stared down at their entwined fingers and squeezed his tight, the desperation clearly etched on her face. She glanced at the table and the files, then at Rafe and Zane.

A heavy sigh escaped her.

"I want to believe that, Noah. But somehow I've got a feeling that the only way we'll find Archimedes is when he finds me first."

LYSSA HAD NEVER seen anything like Noah, Rafe and Zane at work. She tucked her knee under her chin and wrapped her arms round her leg. Their intensity rivaled anything she'd ever witnessed.

Occasionally Noah would glance up at her, meeting her gaze with a worried one of his own. She couldn't stop watching him, and the deep tenor of his voice sent a small shiver up her spine.

While part of her wished he'd let her stay in Chicago, the past few hours had convinced her not to use that code and take off. Despite everything, watching Noah made her believe in the possibility—the possibility of a future.

Should she even allow herself to think that way?

She leaned forward as Noah and Zane rattled off terminology with an ease she'd only witnessed on television.

"Archimedes might be a wacko, but he's a damn good engineer. Check out this design, Noah," Zane said. He pulled apart one of the cameras they'd taken from her apartment. "He's good. I wish I'd dreamed up how he put together the motion- and voice-operated sensors. Efficient, saves size and power. I'm borrowing it."

"Well, when we see him, you can tell him how brilliant you think he is," Noah said. "Can you use the camera to track him?"

Lyssa perked up. Was this it?

"I tried." Zane scowled. "I ended up in the middle of Kandahar when the bouncing finally stopped."

"Somehow, I don't think he's there." A sharp curse escaped from Noah's lips, and he shoved back from the table. "There's got to be a way."

He paced back and forth like a panther in a cage, waiting and wanting to pounce. Lyssa could practically feel the frustration emanating from each step. He settled at the back window and stared outside, his mind obviously whirling with possibilities.

"What about Chastity's notepad?" Lyssa asked.

"No fingerprints," Rafe answered with a frown. "Of course, Archimedes has never left so much as a partial print. The guy is careful."

Rafe was right. Lyssa shoved the files she'd read from cover to cover. "I always thought the feds were hiding something from me. I couldn't believe they didn't have leads that the papers hadn't published, but there's nothing here."

"What about the note Archimedes left for us?" Noah said, still focused on the backyard.

"The infinity symbol matches the other notes he's left on paper," Rafe said.

No one mentioned there were only a few examples of his handwriting. More often than not, Archimedes left his calling card carved into the body.

In fact, Jack had been the first body he'd carved into.

With a quiet shiver, Lyssa forced herself to focus on the here and now, not the past. "What about the other symbol?" Lyssa said. "Can I see it again?"

Rafe pushed the notebook toward her while Zane started in on the laptop again, muttering to himself.

Lyssa studied the pencil drawing Archimedes had created just below the infinity sign. When Noah pulled the chair beside her back and sat next to her, she looked at him. "It's simple. Just a clockwise spiral."

She traced the design with her finger. "It looks familiar but I can't place it." She rubbed the bridge of her nose. "I should know what it means."

"You read the files we have. Has he ever used a second symbol before?"

"Not unless it's in the missing files. The papers didn't have anything about a second drawing either. Not the ones I was able to read."

"Archimedes is waiting for you," Noah said, looking at the message. "Infinity is his signature. So, what is this damn curlicue?"

"I have a feeling if we only knew—"

Noah's phone vibrated. He glanced at the number, stood, then placed the device against his ear.

"Bradford."

Without pause, he crossed the room, away from her. The intensity on his face didn't lessen, and his body moved with primal grace and precision, quiet and deadly. In moments like this he reminded her of Jack. But something more, something even more dangerous to her peace of mind.

With a single glance he looked back at her, two frown lines deepening in his forehead, his expression speculative. Whoever was talking to him hadn't pleased him.

He kept his gaze pinned to her, unmoving and unnerving. Questioning.

A terrifying thought speared into her mind. Her heart hitched.

He couldn't know. No one knew.

Impossible. Noah might be smart and good at his job, but there was no way he'd discovered her secret. Had he?

Oh, God. She'd read his bio; she'd seen his PR photo. She knew he was CEO of three of the top technology companies in the country.

She knew he'd been a marine.

She knew Noah and Jack had spent time together on missions her fiancé couldn't discuss. Noah and Jack couldn't have been more different. Jack had an easy smile, a quiet and trustworthy way about him, despite being a crack sniper.

Noah was forceful, powerful and oddly mysterious. She couldn't pin him down. In contrast, he looked through her as if he could peel away her secrets.

That she refused to allow.

Noah pocketed the phone and Lyssa swallowed the dread.

He walked over to her. "That was Ransom. Reid's stable but not improving. Elijah's going to give it one more day. Ransom promised to put one of his best forensic accountants on the job. He figures this guy's toys cost money. He's looking into suppliers."

Zane got a strange look on his face then hid it just as quickly.

"You know who it is?" Noah asked.

A guilt-ridden expression settled on the computer expert's face. "Maybe. Not something I can talk about."

Noah turned on Zane. "You keeping secrets?"

"Aren't we all?"

"Definitely." Noah sent Lyssa a pointed look. "I think you and I need to talk. Alone."

Oh, boy. She recognized that look, even after only being around him a day. He wanted to know more, and she couldn't tell him everything. She wouldn't.

She possessed one secret she would take to her grave... without hesitation.

A secret she couldn't afford to even think about or she might very well break down. She clutched at Jack's ring, the chain pulling against her neck.

Noah led her out of the main room and into the kitchen. He leaned back against the counter and crossed his arms. "Elijah did a bit of surveillance. He went to Reid's house."

Lyssa stiffened. Reid was the only person who knew, and only because she hadn't had a choice.

"I see you know what I'm talking about."

Lyssa cursed his ability to read her. She had to get better at hiding her feelings and her responses from him. "Can't you just stay out of my head?" she groused.

"I better be good. It's kept me alive." He studied her, not speaking, just staring with an impatient, knowing look.

Sweat beaded on her upper lip. "This is ridiculous. It's simple. Archimedes wants me dead, and I intend to kill him."

"Reid had a file on you at his house. He burned it. Or rather, tried to. Want to tell me why?"

Her throat closed off. This couldn't be happening. She couldn't risk contact, and she refused to panic. Reid would never have given her away. He'd promised her.

"Was the file readable?" She didn't want to ask, but she had to know.

Noah scowled at her.

"No."

She nearly sighed in relief.

"Damn it, Lyssa. I'm trying to save your life." Noah clutched her upper arms.

His imposing six-foot-four-inch presence loomed above her.

"Don't try to intimidate me, Noah Bradford. I won't let you."

She shoved at his chest, and he let her go. She stormed out of the kitchen, panting, and headed straight for her temporary bedroom. She slammed the door closed. Her duffel rested on the bed, untouched.

She could leave, but the truth was, she needed Archimedes dead. Noah Bradford gave her the best chance for that to happen.

Her entire body sagged, uncertainty weighing on her. She rubbed her eyes. She couldn't see a way out. For anyone.

The door cracked open.

She crossed her arms in front of her. "I don't want to talk anymore."

He said nothing but walked over to her, placing his hands on her shoulders, kneading the muscles gently. "I need you to be honest with me, Lyssa. Otherwise, I can't help you." Noah turned her in his arms. "I don't want to fail you." He met her gaze. "And right now, Archimedes has all the advantages."

Her eyes widened at the intensity in his expression. "Oh, my God. You don't think we can win."

"Failure isn't an option," he said, words laced with pent-up frustration. "I don't understand why you're still not being honest. I'm only trying to help."

What could she say? That something more important than herself was at risk?

Someone more important.

"You don't know how to track him," she said. "Despite

all the equipment, Zane, Rafe and even Elijah, Archimedes is still invisible."

"For now." The words dragged out of Noah with distaste, as if he'd chomped on a piece of spoiled fish.

"Thank you for admitting the truth." She stood stiff in his arms, his body strong and sure…and honest, if nothing else.

He tugged her against him and lowered his head to her ear.

"Tell me," he whispered.

His breath caressed the side of her cheek, his strong arms wrapped around her like a cocoon. For the first time in eighteen months she wished she could share the burden.

"I can't," she said.

A single tear ran down her cheek. She pressed her face into Noah's chest. She couldn't let him see the emotion pulsing just beneath the surface.

The past twenty-four hours had given her a glimmer of hope, but she couldn't give anything away.

Not until Archimedes was dead.

Once he was dead, she had a prayer.

Of bringing her baby daughter home.

Chapter Six

Despite her resistance, Noah didn't want to let Lyssa leave his arms. He held her close, too close. She possessed a spine of steel, one he'd never imagined. Noah wanted to shake her, to force her to tell him what she hid. What could be so important that even in the midst of Archimedes's threat, she refused to tell him what Reid knew?

While the operative in Noah cursed her lie of omission, her strength made him want her even more.

Her small convulsive squeeze against him, as if she were clinging to him against her will, gripped his heart. Unwanted emotions bubbled deep within him, feelings he'd quelled the moment he'd realized how much Jack cared for her.

They'd first met Lyssa during a brief assignment at the United Nations. He'd mooned over her from afar. He'd wanted to ask her out, but she'd been too good to be true, so he'd hesitated. Jack had swept in. Game over. Noah had pushed aside the want and taken a few too many overseas assignments so he wouldn't have to face what might have been. He'd been happy for Jack, but the knowledge Noah would never have anyone like Lyssa in his life had haunted him since.

And here she was, in his arms, but he couldn't let himself care now, either.

Noah stepped away from her, but not before he caught the sad look in her eyes. Almost without thinking, he cupped her cheek. Neither of them moved. His heart thudded against his chest and he could barely breathe. Her emerald eyes held him captive, as did her tear-laced lashes. She leaned into his touch for just a moment. Awareness flickered between them. She blinked and cleared her throat. For a moment he wasn't sure if he'd imagined the spark.

She backed away, then fiddled with that duffel, and her gun. Her hands shook a bit.

"Lyssa?"

"Please go," she said, her voice husky, her body's posture screaming at him to leave.

She was right. Getting involved would lead to nothing but distractions and disaster.

He backed away. "Guess I'll get back to the search. If you need anything—"

"You have until tomorrow," Lyssa interrupted softly. "I need something concrete from your team in twenty-four hours or we do things my way." She cut him a quick glance over her shoulder before setting her shotgun on the bed. "I have no choice."

In other words, back to Chicago, back to placing a giant target on her back. She'd told him more than he wanted to know. She had no faith in him, and she was willing to die to catch Archimedes.

Well, he wouldn't let her.

Noah shut the door on her and stalked into the living room. Zane looked up, speculation on his face.

"She's given us one day. Then she's going back to Chicago to wait him out."

"Damn," Rafe muttered.

"I like her," Zane said.

Noah rounded on Zane then caught the gleam in the man's eye.

"I thought so," Zane said. "You gonna be able to stay focused, Noah?"

He let a curse fly at them and riffled through the files. There had to be something he was missing. Some clue to this guy's identity.

Beethoven's Fifth sounded from Noah's phone. He grabbed the cell. "What's wrong, Dad?"

He ignored his friends' shocked expressions.

"Noah," Paul Bradford's voice came through the receiver. "Are you safe?"

"I'm fine."

His father let out a relieved sigh. "Thank God."

"What are you talking about?" Noah asked, perplexed.

His phone beeped again.

His chief operating officer's number popped onto the screen, along with a 911 code. What the hell was going on?

"Hold on, Dad." He put his father on hold. "Bradford."

A fit of coughing sounded through the phone. "We got problems, Noah. Maybe terrorism. Someone tried to gas everyone in the building. Something went through the ventilation system. Dozens of people heading to the hospital. A few are in critical condition. Reporters are everywhere."

Noah raced over to the television and flipped it to a national news channel. He stared at the screen. A helicopter flew over an all-too-familiar building.

"Are you okay, Crystal?"

"I'll survive." His old math teacher's hacking through the phone told Noah otherwise.

"Get to the hospital. I'm sending some security personnel to help you." Noah nodded at Rafe, who picked up the phone. Within minutes, Ransom would send a couple of CTC operatives to get things under control.

"We need you here, Noah," Crystal said, her voice fading. "Where are you?"

"I'm getting someone out there, Crystal. I…" His voice trailed off. Damn it. They needed him. He stared at the closed bedroom door. So did Lyssa.

He shoved his hand through his hair. "Get to the doctor, Crystal. Help is on its way. I'll call you back."

Noah's arm fell to his side. Chaotic images flashed on the screen. A flood of people fled the manufacturing plant in Silicon Valley like a stampede. *His* people.

Police, fire engines, paramedics, ambulances, hazmat trucks and a bevy of flashing lights filled the parking lots surrounding Dreamcatcher Technologies, Inc.

The corporation had become synonymous with innovative and affordable surveillance and encryption hardware and software. *His* company. *His* dream. *His* friends and colleagues.

"Noah? Noah!"

His father's voice shouted through the phone's receiver. Noah lifted the device to his ear. "I'm here, Dad. I'm watching the news. I'm okay."

"Thank God. Where are you?"

"Not where I should be," Noah said quietly.

"Noah Bradford, president and CEO, could not be reached for comment," a faceless newscaster droned. "Hospitals have been overrun with patients. No word on the cause of the explosion."

"Yeah, like you even tried." Noah scowled at the television screen.

"Crystal Lawson, COO, indicated that Homeland Security and the FBI had been contacted. In the meantime, federal, state and local authorities have been notified. Areas surrounding the Dreamcatcher plant have been evacuated. Terrorism has not been ruled out."

The camera panned the sky.

Noah stilled.

A huge black symbol had been painted on the roof of the building.

Infinity.

"Archimedes," he said gnashing his teeth together. He met Rafe's and Zane's gazes. "Dad, I want you to listen carefully to me. Get out of your house. Contact everyone. The whole family needs to disappear for a while."

"What's going on, Noah?"

"Do you see that symbol on top of the building? The infinity? That's Archimedes's symbol. If he's targeted my company, I don't want him to target…" Noah couldn't finish the sentence.

"The serial killer?" His father gasped. "What—? Never mind. I think I know. I'll make sure the family is safe."

The bedroom door cracked open. Lyssa walked out, her pale face showing her devastation. She'd obviously heard. She strode to him and clutched his arm. Her wide eyes stared at the screen.

"Don't take any chances, Dad. Don't search the internet. Don't even get online. Don't go anywhere you can be tracked. Drive, don't fly. This guy is smart. He did this to make a point. I couldn't stand it if anything happened to any of you because of me."

"Noah." His father's voice was quiet. "Come home."

"I can't," Noah said, hating the thickness in his voice. "He's probably watching. Just make sure everyone's safe. Especially Emily.

"And tell Mitch…tell Mitch I'm sorry."

What else could he say?

Lyssa leaned into him, slipping her fingers through his free hand, squeezing tight. He didn't try to stop himself.

He pulled her close against him; she was one of the few people who understood what he felt.

He could handle the danger to himself. He couldn't handle his family being a target.

"I have to go, Dad."

"Noah…" His father paused. "You catch this bastard, yeah?"

"Yeah."

Noah ended the call and continued watching the screen. "That son of a bitch."

Lyssa gripped his hand tighter. "God, I'm sorry. This is my—"

"Don't go there, Lyssa. I know exactly who's to blame." His gaze snapped to Zane and then to Rafe. "Check every flight from Chicago to San Jose Airport. Get me a lead. If he's ramped up his game then so do we."

Noah tugged Lyssa to the table that served as their war room and sat her down. "Let's go over every detail one more time. In your first interviews about Archimedes you described him. You said he was a man, not too old, a little under six feet? Right?"

"I never saw his face. He didn't move like he'd been trained. Not like you or Jack." She gripped Noah's fingers. "I *still* don't understand how he got the drop on Jack. He wasn't that strong or fast. He couldn't catch me when I ran."

"He doesn't use his body, he uses his mind. That's how we have to catch him. He leaves a calling card. He's an arrogant SOB."

Noah opened a couple of files. "Not one of his victims was bruised or battered. They weren't killed with his bare hands."

He leaned back in the chair. "We need to set a trap. On our terms."

"But how?" Lyssa tucked her knee under her. "At my apartment?"

"He knows me," Noah mused. "He's trying to scare me off. Once my family is safe, we take this fight to Denver. On *my* home turf. He wants a fight, he's getting one."

LYSSA PRESSED THE door closed on her small bedroom. The lock clicked shut, muffling the continued tapping of computer keys. She didn't turn on the overhead light in the dimming room but sagged against the wood. Her head ached, her eyes burned with fatigue from staring at papers and a computer screen all day.

They'd found nothing. For hours she'd worked beside Rafe, Zane and Noah as they'd analyzed file after file, data stream after data stream.

In the midst of word that CTC had people on the ground in Silicon Valley, that Noah's COO suffered from lung damage but would probably recover, Noah had used a few screwdrivers and what looked like parts from an electronics store to jury-rig a supercharged communications jammer.

Seriously, the man's capability scared her. All of them did.

The team had accessed street cameras in front of her Chicago apartment and work building, and in front of Noah's business. They ran images through a facial-recognition software program.

No results.

Zane had done some sort of voodoo and now a computer program weeded through passenger lists from flights to Chicago and those between the city and San Jose. The only person they'd recognized so far was Reid on his flight from D.C.

She hadn't felt quite so useless in a long time. Not since

she'd walked into a gun range after the first attack to learn how to take care of herself. She could do very little except wade through that horrifying series of files and look over lists of names and faces.

Not that it had helped.

She'd only known three victims: Jack, Chastity and Reid.

At least Reid was holding his own. So far.

Her shoulders rounded in weariness, Lyssa crossed the room and turned on a small bedside lamp. Her duffel remained on her bed, and she dug into the bottom. She pulled out two books, journals she'd started after going stir-crazy her first month in protective custody.

She might not be able to manipulate ones and zeros like Zane and Noah, but she'd been face to stocking mask with Archimedes. Had she forgotten some small detail, something from the night Archimedes had killed Jack?

Or maybe the second attack.

The one that had terrified her even more than witnessing Jack's death.

With a shudder, she sat on the bed cross-legged and paged through the first book. The memories overwhelmed her.

If her baby girl hadn't been with the babysitter…the thought gave her nightmares practically every night. But the terror had given her the strength to do something she'd never believe she'd be capable of.

She hadn't seen Jocelyn in seventeen months, twenty days and four hours. With Reid unconscious, only Jocelyn's temporary mother and Lyssa could reveal the truth.

If Archimedes killed her, at least Lyssa would take the secret of Jocelyn to her grave. Her daughter would be safe.

Lyssa had sacrificed everything for her baby girl. She'd sacrifice her life without hesitation.

Archimedes could never ever find out about Jocelyn.

But, Noah had, in the small corner of her mind, reignited a spark of hope that Archimedes could be caught, that he would pay, so Lyssa forced herself to read on.

After hiding the journal in the bedside table, Lyssa sighted the shotgun at the picture hanging on the wall.

She could imagine Archimedes standing there, only his eyes and mouth visible.

A small squeeze and it would be over.

If Noah could find him.

A soft knock sounded. She laid down the weapon. "Yes?"

Noah eased open the door, his muscular figure filling the entrance. He stepped into the dim bedroom. "How are you doing?"

"Like I won't ever find the needle in the haystack." She tugged out a box of shells hidden beneath a set of pajamas. "He's out there somewhere. God knows what he's doing, who he's hurting."

"May I?"

He held out his hands and she placed the weapon in them. He pointed the gun's barrel to the floor, testing the weight in his hands. "Impressive," Noah said. "Quite a recoil?"

"I'm used to it." She shrugged. "The barrel is short. I like the front grip for stability. It's loud, and he'll hear it and see it coming. He won't be getting up."

"Where do you keep it?"

"Under my pillow." She didn't blink. "If he ever gets in, I'll be ready."

"He's fixated on you. You realize that," Noah said, sitting on the bed, returning the shotgun.

"I'm hoping the gun gives me the advantage. All I need is a clear shot, Noah. I won't hesitate."

"I don't want him to get that close to you."

What could she say? That she hoped Archimedes *did* find her, and soon, so she could end the wait.

Placing the empty weapon at her side, waiting to be loaded, she looked up at Noah. "How is your family?"

"Safe for the moment."

Noah's eyes darkened with worry.

"Maybe you should go to them—" The words had to be said.

"I'm not leaving you. My brother Mitch was SWAT. My dad was a cop. They know how to protect themselves."

Lyssa twisted her fingers. "I'm so sorry they got dragged into this. If I thought it would help, I'd go back to Chicago." She sighed. "It wouldn't help, would it?"

"He knows I'm involved, and he's not happy about it. I've got my other companies on a security alert. They're taking all the precautions they can." Noah scooted closer to her and placed his hand on her knee. "Count on one thing, I won't leave your side until he's no longer a threat."

With a sad smile, she covered his hand with hers. He couldn't look away from her green eyes. So much hurt, so much pain, and yet a determination that wouldn't quit. He turned his hand and squeezed hers, offering comfort.

She gnawed on her lip, her nerves showing through. He couldn't look away. The desire that had been flickering through him since he'd seen her again ignited into a flame. He was so close to her that if he leaned over just a bit, their lips would touch.

If he ever kissed her, he didn't know if he'd be able to stop.

"Noah," she said softly, her voice questioning, her eyes wide with something he didn't want to identify.

His hand drifted down her arm, and she shivered under his touch. She leaned forward. The glittering diamond from Jack's engagement ring against her breastbone caught the light.

Noah took a calming breath and scooted back. "Rest," he said, rising. With a last long, slow look he left the room.

Once he closed the door of her small bedroom, away from the lavender scent that lingered, he sighed, willing his racing heart to calm.

"She okay?" Rafe walked over and nodded at the room.

Noah studied the man who'd saved his life on more missions than he could count, the man who had sacrificed more than anyone could possibly know. The man who knew him better than anyone. Even his family.

They may know he'd joined the Marine Corps., but they had no idea of the missions he'd gone on…the ones deep into enemy territory.

At first the secrets had been part of the job. Then it had morphed into protecting them from worrying, especially after his father's accident. Now it had become a way of life—keeping that barrier up so no one could see inside him.

Who would want to?

"She's pretending," he admitted finally.

"Don't we all?"

The corners of Noah's lips lifted. "Oh, yeah. You ever get tired of it?"

Rafe closed his eyes, regret clear on his expression. Rafe let very few see beneath his mask. He and Noah were kindred spirits that way.

"I paid the price. You just go on. It's all you can do."

Noah glanced at the room where he'd left Lyssa. His arms itched to hold her, to do way more than that, but giving in to wants and needs almost never turned out well. "She's thinking about running again. To protect us."

"You gotta love that about her."

Noah narrowed his gaze. "You *like* her?"

"What's not to like?" Rafe said. "She's determined, gorgeous and knows how to use a gun. Zane's got a crush on her. I've half fallen for her, too. My kind of girl."

Noah glared at him. Rafe raised his hands. "And taken. I got that."

"She's in love with a dead man," Noah said quietly. "She wears his ring around her neck."

"A dead man can't hold her in his arms. You have a distinct advantage, my friend."

"Not possible." Noah crossed the room and opened one of the files, deliberately changing the subject. "Archimedes has the upper hand. He's got eyes and ears at Justice."

"You know what we have to do," Rafe said, fiddling with his patch.

"Yeah." Noah's jaw throbbed. "Make her vulnerable. We're doing exactly what she wanted in the first place and more. It ticks me off."

"Want Zane to start dropping bread crumbs?"

Noah closed his eyes. "I want to encase her in bubble wrap and put her in the middle of Antarctica."

"Have you figured out what she's hiding yet?" Rafe asked.

"No. But whatever it is, Reid knew. And they've both taken a lot of risks to hide it." Noah studied the closed door. "Let's hope Archimedes never finds out, because if it's important to Lyssa, he'll go after it."

FIRE CRACKLED IN the fireplace, its glow eerie in the completely dark hotel room. The flicker sent shadowy tongues up the wall.

Archimedes—God, he loved the name the press had given him—watched the images play through the large television screen he'd connected through his laptop. He'd replayed it seventy-three times so far.

Alessandra. And *that* man.

Noah Bradford.

He zoomed in to their clutched hands. He'd memorized every second. The tightening of her fingers on Bradford, her leaning into him.

The man's eyes following her every movement.

But, more importantly, Alessandra's blatant desire. She wanted him, too.

This couldn't be happening.

The stemmed glass shattered in his hand, red wine exploding and splattering onto the floor.

He rose from his chair, ignoring a mess for the first time that he could remember, but Alessandra needed his attention.

She couldn't be this weak.

He tugged out his tablet and tapped a few keys.

A red dot blinked.

Still in Texas.

Bradford's plane hadn't taken off to California. He was still with her.

Archimedes knew the next step. He would have to pay them a visit—make sure Alessandra focused on her destiny, on her journey to become worthy of their life together.

She was his destiny.

He was going to prove it to her.

NOAH HADN'T SLEPT all night. He twirled the small screwdriver in his fingers and scowled at the tiny pieces of Archimedes's camera lying on the table.

Everything about the gadget was generic; nothing could be traced.

"Please, no. Please don't!"

Lyssa's screams echoed through the house.

Noah sprung to his feet, palmed his Glock and ran into the hallway. He slammed open Lyssa's door and rushed into her room.

Her body twisted under a single sheet, her hands in fists, her face damp with perspiration.

He felt Zane and Rafe's presence behind him. One slight glance showed their guns were drawn and ready.

"Nightmare," Noah whispered hurrying to her bed. "Close the door."

They nodded, sympathy in their eyes, and the lock clicked, shutting him in with Lyssa.

He sat on the bed and gathered her into his arms.

Tears streamed down her face. With a gentle touch, he stroked her cheek. "Lyssa, it's just a dream."

Her mouth twisted in fury. "I'll kill you. I won't let you hurt us!"

Her head shook back and forth against his chest. She punched at Noah, but he held her fast. He bent closer, his voice soft and low. "Shh, honey. It's not real."

The trouble was, her nightmares could very well become real.

She whimpered and slowly settled in his arms. Her eyes blinked; she looked up at him. Swiping at her tears, she stared around the room. "What, where—?"

"You called out in your sleep," he said, pushing her hair back from her face.

She grew pale. "What did I say?"

The vulnerability in her eyes twisted his heart. "You wanted Archimedes dead."

"That's true." She scooted away from Noah, running her hands through her tousled hair. "I'm sorry I woke you."

"I wasn't sleeping," he said softly. "I was tinkering a bit."

He forced himself not to follow his instincts, not to cuddle her close and use his lips and body to make her forget.

He shouldn't be feeling this way. She was too vulnerable; she'd wrapped her arms around herself, that protective posture one huge defense. But he couldn't stop the need or the flames that had kindled with every moment near her. He'd dreamed about her for the past few years; he'd compared every woman he'd dated to the woman sitting just a few feet from him. And now they were alone in a bedroom in the dark.

She clutched the sheet into her fists. "I dream of him. Every night. Of changing the past. Of killing him and stopping all of this." She met his gaze. "What kind of person does that make me, to want another person dead? To want to kill him so badly that I can see it, feel it, do it in my dreams?"

He pried her fingers open, her palms speckled with red nail marks. He stroked the damaged flesh. "Archimedes hurt you. Your mind wants to fix it."

She didn't scoot away, just gazed up at Noah. "Two years ago, I didn't even own a gun. Now I can shoot and not flinch. Two years ago, my biggest problem was choosing a wedding dress and hoping that when the Russian president made a statement, that my translation wouldn't cause an international incident. Now I look over my shoulder everywhere I go. I can't trust anyone. I can't tell anyone the truth about my life or my past.

"I can't live this way anymore."

Noah slid to her side and pulled her head to his shoulder, stroking her back. "It will be over soon."

"Even when it's finally over, I'll never be the same. Have I lost my soul?" she whispered. "Am I just an empty shell?"

How many times had Noah asked himself that question? While Lyssa dreamed of taking the law into her own hands, he'd done it. He'd been judge, jury and executioner. Sometimes there was no choice.

He tilted her chin up and sank into the distraught green sea of her eyes. "You know what I see? A woman who wants to survive, who cares about the people around her. Who wants to stop a man who cares nothing about anyone else." His hand drifted under her jawline to toy with a curl of her hair. "I see a woman who cares more for others than herself."

A reminiscent smile tugged at her lips. "That's something Jack would have said."

The words shredded Noah's heart. Jack. It was Jack she cared about. She still loved Noah's best friend.

And that fact hurt like hell. God, what he wouldn't give for someone to love him this much.

What he wouldn't give for Lyssa to… He cleared his throat. "I'd better let you get some sleep."

"Don't leave. I can't take any more nightmares." She burrowed closer into him. "So tired."

Inside he groaned, but he settled on top of the covers, dragging his finger down her arm. "I'm not letting you out of my sight, Lyssa. I promise you that."

He pulled her covers over her and her tired eyes blinked up at him.

"Sleep," he said, stroking the soft strands of her hair. "We have some planning to do tomorrow."

Her eyelids lifted. "As much as part of me thinks you should leave, I'm glad you're here, Noah."

She closed her eyes.

Noah didn't move. He didn't dare. Carefully, he set his gun on the nightstand.

Lyssa, here in his arms. Not quite how he'd imagined it.

A small sigh escaped her and she shifted even closer, showing him a trust she guarded so carefully.

If only she would trust him so much during the light of day.

SUNLIGHT PIERCED THROUGH the shutters. Lyssa groaned against the bright assault and turned over.

A large body stopped her.

Noah.

Memories of last night roared back. She flushed and peeked over at him. He lay sprawled on top of the covers, the top of his jeans unbuttoned, exhaustion painting his features.

Carefully, she rolled to the other side of the bed and rose. She hadn't taken two steps when a voice stopped her.

"Don't bother sneaking out," he muttered without opening his eyes. "You tiptoe with the subtlety of a herd of elephants."

So much for saving face. "I need coffee."

"Make mine black," he said, burying his head in the pillow.

Lyssa slipped into the hallway. Zane sat at the computer, his hair sticking straight up. "You been up all night?"

He removed his earphones. "Mostly. Narrowed the search down to one thousand, three hundred twenty-three possible suspects on flights yesterday."

Rafe sat on the sofa, his 1911 by his side. The twenty-four-hour news channel flickered in the early morning, its sound muted.

"Did that snowstorm hit last night?" Lyssa asked. She walked to the front door heading to the enclosed screen porch.

"Don't!" Rafe shouted. "Let me go first."

She'd already turned the knob.

The door eased toward her without the slightest tug, a heavy weight slowly coming at her.

She jumped back.

A body tumbled into the foyer, then rolled onto its back.

Noah leaped in front of Rafe tackling her to the ground. Lyssa looked from underneath Noah's arm at the distorted face.

"Oh, God. I know him!"

Chapter Seven

Noah covered Lyssa's body with his, curving his body to protect her. As if reading his mind, Rafe jumped over them, weapon in hand, and slammed the front door behind him. Zane raced to the back door.

Noah rolled Lyssa away from the body, their legs tangled. "Get your gun," he shouted. "Barricade yourself in."

She didn't hesitate. She sprinted to the bedroom. Hoping she'd stay put but not counting on it, Noah rushed into the garage. He slid beneath the SUV. No explosives. Using his fingertips, he checked along the garage door. No tampering. Finally he studied the garage-door opener. A guy like Archimedes liked gadgets. No sign he'd been inside.

The realization didn't relax Noah one bit. He strode into the house. Lyssa had planted herself not two feet from the man's body, her shotgun pointed at the door.

"Clear!" Zane's voice filtered from the back.

She spun around, her eyes narrow with deadly intent. She stilled when she noticed him standing there.

Her body stood poised, ready to fire.

"Clear!" Noah shouted.

She gripped the weapon tighter.

Seconds later, Rafe gave a final yell. "Clear!"

Everyone had checked in. She allowed the barrel to lower a bit.

"Got something!" Rafe's voice sounded from outside.

"Come on, honey," Noah said, holding out his hand. "I'm not letting you out of my sight."

She placed her hand in his.

"Keep ready," he called. "We're coming out."

Anchoring Lyssa to his side, he ran out front, meeting Zane, as the computer expert rounded the side corner.

Zane squatted down and picked up the small electronic device. "A jammer. Nice work."

Noah scowled at him. Zane shrugged. "He may be a psychopath, but he's damn good at what he does. He disabled the motion detectors on the front porch and blocked the signal of the video cameras I set up." Zane frowned. "I thought that design was foolproof."

"It should have been," Noah said, ticking through the possible vulnerabilities in his company's number-one-selling camera. "Bring it," he said as he made his way to the screened porch. He studied the slit on the screen door. Smears of blood dotted the metal mesh. "Arrogant SOB just pranced in."

Lyssa scanned the surroundings. Everything inside Noah wanted her back in the house, but he couldn't risk it. God knew where Archimedes was. Noah ran his hand across the motion detectors. He met the worried looks of both Rafe and Zane. They understood.

"He could have waltzed in," Lyssa said, raising her weapon again. "He could be here now."

Rafe lowered his voice. "He could have burned this place down in minutes with that accelerant he uses. We're damn lucky."

"I don't like counting on luck," Noah said. "How did he find us?"

Another search of the surroundings and the interior, and he breathed somewhat easier.

They secured all entries, including the damaged front porch, before returning inside.

Lyssa stood above the victim's body, still grasping her weapon, a guilt-ridden expression on her face. "Oh, Frederick. What have I done?"

"Who is he?" Noah asked, kneeling beside the body. Archimedes had used an old French Foreign Legion *loupe,* a double coil of steel, to strangle Frederick. The wire had cut into his throat. Effective, quick and silent.

"My first boss," Lyssa said, her voice shaking.

Noah glanced up at her. Her eyes flashed not with fear but with anger. He didn't know which he preferred at this point. Anger caused mistakes; desperation made those mistakes even more likely.

"He gave me a chance to be a translator at the United Nations right out of grad school," she said. "He really believed in me." She bit the corner of her lip, the pressure causing the edge to turn white. "It was my first permanent job, my first real home after moving constantly because of my father's job at the State Department."

Sorrow laced her expression, but she shoved it away. Her grip squeezed the weapon even tighter. He had to admire her grit.

"I haven't seen him since I went into WitSec."

If only Noah could protect Lyssa from this latest dose of reality, but Archimedes left no room for shielding her from their situation's true vulnerability. Noah's only choice was to outsmart a killer who seemed to have the drop on them. At least for the moment.

Noah studied the body. Archimedes had left the man's shirt opened down the front to reveal his handiwork. A knife had sliced across the poor guy's midsection. Noah eased back the material with the barrel of his gun.

No infinity. Unusual.

Archimedes had carved a different symbol into Frederick's belly.

The psycho had left a bar-shaped wound across his abdomen. Above the thin rectangle, he'd burned three geometrically perfect circles, the edges scorched. Even now, an odor of singed flesh lingered.

"Looks like acid of some kind," Noah said finally. "Elijah would be able to tell for sure. Send him some detailed photos and a sample."

"I don't recall anything comparable in the Archimedes files we have," Rafe said.

"Nothing similar ever made it into the papers," Lyssa added, her hand over her mouth. "God. Why would he do this?"

"Another message. Someone else you know," Noah bit out. "More importantly, he knows where we are."

"I'm tired of this. Why doesn't he just give me an invitation to where he wants me to die?" Lyssa said, her voice rising.

With a sharp glance at her, Noah stood, blocking her view of the body. "He wants you to figure it out. He's courting you. And with his latest *offering* he's taking you back to the past. To when he first met you."

"Jack's murder. While I was working at the UN."

"Exactly." Noah stroked the stubble on his chin. Retreat hadn't worked. Confrontation would have to. "Change of plans. We go back to the past, back to when you worked for the UN. Back to where Jack died."

"Connecticut." Lyssa's face paled and she clutched at her necklace. "God, no."

ANOTHER CURSE ESCAPED Rafe in the Dallas rush-hour traffic. Lyssa couldn't blame him. The unusual cold front hadn't shut down the Texas roads, but Southern drivers couldn't be trusted on icy highways. Especially those in big trucks with delusions of safety.

Lyssa peered through the strangely dim light.

"How's the weather?" Rafe asked.

Noah tapped his phone. "Storm front's moving in. We need to hurry if we're going to beat it."

"Tell that to all these idiots."

The traffic slowed to a crawl. Lyssa couldn't stop her leg from bouncing, her nerves on edge. Twenty-four hours and Archimedes had tracked them down. The reality had quashed the last flicker of hope surviving inside her.

If Noah couldn't help her, no one could. To keep her baby girl safe, no choices remained. Lyssa would have to let Archimedes find her.

She would die.

But her baby would have a life. That's all that mattered anymore. Her heart ached with the truth. She'd let Jack down; she'd let herself down. Except in one way.

Archimedes didn't know about her daughter.

It would stay that way.

She would miss her little girl's first day of school, her high school graduation, her college graduation, her wedding, but her daughter would survive. She'd be loved.

Lyssa had picked the perfect person to be Jocelyn's mother. Someday, it might be safe to reveal the truth. Someday...when Archimedes was dead.

The lane to their left began to move. A man barked into his phone and drummed his fingers on his steering wheel. A woman chanced a look every few seconds in the mirror while putting on lipstick, then eyeliner. A frenzied mom wore pajamas, her unadorned face and four kids in the backseat providing its own tale.

All normal lives. All easy to read.

She stole a glance at Noah. His gaze burrowed into her,

unflinching. He'd been watching her, his expression speculative, as if he could see right into her mind.

Knowing she couldn't allow him any closer—for her sake as much as for his safety—she turned away from him.

He confused her. On so many levels.

A snippet of memory flashed through her. She'd encountered Noah via her UN job, but barely. Once she'd started dating Jack, Noah had vanished for the most part. The few times they'd met, she hadn't been able to pin him down. She'd said so to Jack.

He'd chuckled. *Yeah, Noah's an enigma, all right. First day of boot camp, he shows up—the only one who's actually got millions in the bank—and not because he inherited. He ripped through the* New York Times *crossword puzzle in less than a half hour, made everyone look like an idiot during class, so a couple guys thought they'd teach the ubergeek a lesson. I stepped forward, figured he'd need a hand. Noah had them on the ground in seconds. He didn't need me. Didn't need anyone, really.* Jack had kissed her palm. *Noah's the best there is, but he likes to work alone. He's too smart, too good at what he does. I can't think of one weakness in him, except he can't stop trying to prove himself. It's like he's fighting demons that don't exist.*

She saw the truth of Jack's words now. And they scared her. Noah wouldn't stop until he succeeded. Or Archimedes killed him. Noah would never let her fight the battle on her own.

Lyssa would have to find a way.

"Archimedes located us too fast," Rafe commented. He expertly darted into the right lane toward the exit leading to Lancaster Regional Airport. "CTC owns the safe house. Has he made the connection?"

"We're either being traced," Noah said, "or he's tunneled through Zane's system at CTC. Take your pick."

The man in the front seat grumbled. "I swept the place for tracking and listening devices. And CTC is locked up tight. I don't get it."

"Beef up the tracking receiver—"

Noah didn't have time to finish the order before Zane held up a screwdriver. "I'm on it. This guy is pissing me off."

"I want the plane and everything on it scanned before we take off," Noah said, his voice curt. His fingers clutched his Glock.

The weight of her .45 in its holster didn't relax her one bit. Lyssa had the unbearable feeling Archimedes could jump out of anywhere at any moment.

"The guy's big on symbolism," Rafe said, his voice wondering. "All these weird icons…plus Frederick."

"Frederick was obvious." Noah's hand tightened on the butt of the gun. "He gave Lyssa the opportunity to speak, and his throat was cut—"

"My translator job. Archimedes shut him up." Lyssa wrapped her arms around her body, a chill from the inside taking over. "Why now? I haven't been back to the UN since the night Jack was killed."

"A warning to those who help you perhaps," Noah speculated. "And much more straightforward than whatever those two symbols represent."

Noah, Rafe, Zane and Elijah were helping her. She'd made everything worse. Now the only way out was to somehow beat Archimedes at his game. To decipher his message. The designs meant something, but she had no idea what. She rolled the images through her mind. The spiral; the bar and circles.

"Something to do with math or engineering?" Lyssa asked.

"I see where you're going. He probably likes being called Archimedes after the Greek mathematician and engineer," Noah said as he searched the surrounding vehicles, not even meeting her gaze. "Neither symbols are used in math or electrical engineering. The original Archimedes determined the value of pi. That's related to the golden spiral, but it's a stretch."

Lyssa stared over at him, dumbstruck.

Rafe crossed the lanes of traffic quickly. "Noah's sort of like a human computer of useless math trivia. Good thing he has other, more worthwhile talents."

"Just drive." Noah peered out the back of the SUV.

Lyssa recognized Noah's tension. She understood. They had no solid leads; Archimedes had found them. He was winning.

No one said a word the rest of the drive until finally Rafe pulled into the private airport. He honked the horn three times.

At the signal, a large door to one of the hangars slid open. A pushback tug exited the building, pulling the Lear slowly into the daylight.

"We should be able to take her up soon," Noah said.

The two vehicles rolled out onto the tarmac then stopped.

Noah exited the car, his gun at the ready. Rafe and Zane peered around the deserted airport.

Nobody else would have dared come out with the weather worsening.

Lyssa slid from her seat. Tension knotted the base of her neck.

Everything looked normal, if not eerily desolate.

Noah opened the rear of the SUV. "Let's—"

An explosion erupted from the belly of the plane. Flames soared into the sky, engulfing the Lear in fire. Shrapnel flew in every direction.

Noah leaped at Lyssa, shoved her to the ground and rolled her under the SUV. Her body pounded into the asphalt, scraping her palms and side.

Fiery debris flew at them. She ducked her head down as metal pelted the car.

"Stay here," Noah shouted at Zane.

The man nodded and positioned himself between Lyssa and the plane.

She gazed at the hellfire that had erupted. Mini explosions sent more burning metal soaring at them. Several pieces bounced off the tarmac, and one hit Lyssa in the arm. She slapped it away, and Zane doused the licks of fire that took hold of her wool coat.

Rafe and Noah raced toward the tug. Just as they reached it, a ball of fire barreled near the gas tank. The back end erupted into flames.

Black smoke billowed into the sky, and Lyssa squinted through the blaze. The man inside the tug had slumped over the steering wheel, unconscious. "The driver!" she shouted.

Noah yanked at the door, but it didn't budge. Rafe rounded the vehicle to try the other side, but that one wouldn't open either. Frantically, Noah looked around. He grabbed a metal rod and slammed it through the glass. It shattered. Noah reached inside.

He didn't see the fire that swept toward him.

"Noah, look out!" Lyssa screamed.

They didn't hesitate. Noah shoved his shoulders through the hole in the glass and yanked the driver through. Rafe climbed up beside Noah. Together they dragged the man from the truck, falling back onto the tarmac.

Sparks erupted.

"Cover your head," Zane yelled.

Lyssa buried her head in her arms just as another explosion hit.

Noah and Rafe fell to their knees, the driver between them.

Sirens closed in on them. The driver rolled to his back and propped himself up. "What happened?" he asked, coughing. He held his bleeding head then looked up at the burning plane. "Oh, man, did I do that?"

"It wasn't your fault," Lyssa said from beneath the SUV. "It was mine."

Noah wiped the soot from his face. "No, it wasn't. We know who's to blame, don't we?" He turned to the driver. "Did you see anyone around the plane, anyone unusual around the tarmac today?"

The guy shook his head and doubled over into another fit of coughing. "It's been dead with the ice storm heading this way. Just some inspector."

Lyssa caught the expression Noah shot at Rafe. "Archimedes?" she asked.

"I'm on it." Rafe said, rising to his feet, heading for the hangar.

Fire engines screamed to a stop, and firefighters tugged their hoses out to douse the blaze. Noah knelt beside the SUV. "Stay there," he said to her. "Too many people around. I don't want you seen."

Unwilling to argue, she hunkered down. "I'm sorry about your plane."

He crouched beside the SUV, gun in his hand. "Like I said, not your fault." He tilted his head and squinted. "What the—? Zane, see that white paint next to the plane. Can you make it out?"

Lyssa's breath hung in her throat. "What is it?"

Without answering, Noah rose slightly. He scanned the area, and Lyssa couldn't stop the shiver from skittering through her body. Noah's gaze narrowed, his expression deadly.

Above Lyssa, the SUV creaked as Zane climbed to the roof.

"Well?" Noah asked.

Lyssa couldn't see anything from her hiding place.

"Another message." Zane pulled out his weapon.

"Infinity?" Noah asked.

"No. This time it's an epsilon."

ARCHIMEDES HAD TO admit Noah Bradford had good taste in planes. He gripped the arm of the luxurious seat of the Lear. So similar to Noah's custom-built plane. The plane that now burned to nothingness.

The immaculate interior couldn't be faulted. Not an item out of place. He should purchase a chair made of the supple leather.

He pressed the microfiber cloth against the screen of his tablet, removing the thumbprint, then typed in the web address he used to route his cameras.

Chaos ruled the screen.

Fire, flashing lights, shouts.

With a flick of his finger he adjusted the camera's angle. The lens zeroed in on Noah Bradford. The man stood staring at the latest message.

Where was Alessandra?

He panned once again.

Just two of the men Archimedes hadn't been able to identify. Yet.

Then he noted a small figure underneath the SUV. He zoomed in.

There she was.

He couldn't see her face.

Archimedes gripped the tablet tight. He wanted to witness that flash of comprehension. She *had* to understand his message. Once she deciphered the symbols, she'd know the truth—that they were meant to be. That he was the only one who understood how intelligent, how perfect, she really was.

A figure blocked her from view.

Noah Bradford had crouched down, staring directly into the camera. Within seconds the signal ceased.

"He's smart. Too smart, maybe."

Archimedes drummed his fingers then punched the intercom. "Change of destination. Take me to Denver, Colorado." He lifted his finger. "I have a message to deliver. Personally."

STRIPS OF SLEET pounded the airport, washing away any evidence—not that Noah believed Archimedes had tipped his hand.

With Rafe doing another perimeter check and Zane checking the camera they'd spotted, Noah refused to leave Lyssa. She sat in the SUV, huddled in her threadbare coat. He needed to get her another. The temperature had fallen to match that of Chicago.

"No doubt he's watching and laughing," Noah muttered, lifting the hood of his jacket to keep the ice from his face.

Zane walked over to him, a small camera in his latex-covered hand. Noah recognized the signature build all too well. "Archimedes."

Rafe came up behind Zane. "We're clear."

"Yeah, well, every time we think that," Noah said, "the guy makes his presence known again."

"He used C-4 on the plane in several locations," Rafe

said. "Detonators were something I've never seen before. Neither had the bomb squad."

"Why doesn't that surprise me?" Noah pulled his phone from his pocket. "I'm calling for new transportation. And this time it won't be tied to me."

He dialed a number.

Immediately, Ransom Grainger picked up. "I heard about the explosion. What do you need?"

Noah shouldn't have been surprised. "The guy knows where we are. He's one step ahead of us."

"You've checked for tracking devices?"

"Of course. But this guy has some serious technical skills. Even Zane is impressed."

Ransom whistled. "Okay. I'll send a plane to you. Why not bring Lyssa here?"

"He doesn't know about CTC and I want to keep it that way." Noah lowered his voice. "I can't risk anyone there."

"What do you want to do?" Ransom asked.

"I'll send you his latest puzzle. Three symbols. We're not sure what they mean, but the last body he delivered— that was a man from Lyssa's past. Archimedes wants us to go to Connecticut. Back where it all started. I don't have any other options."

Tapping fingers sounded through the phone. "Jack's home is still empty. With this economy, it's stayed on the market."

"I know." A curse erupted from him. "Damn it, we're playing right into his hands."

Ransom didn't speak for a moment. "I've never heard your emotions get the better of you, Falcon. What's going on?"

Noah sighed and cast a glance at Lyssa then with a signal to Rafe to watch her, walked just inside the hangar, out of sight. "Jack and I were scheduled to go on one last job before he retired. Jack refused and our commanding officer *requested* me to convince him. He thought we needed Jack's skills."

"You didn't call?"

"Oh, I called all right…instead of showing up at his door like I should have. Jack asked me to come by the next day. He could charm a caffeine addict into giving up his morning coffee."

"It was that night, wasn't it?" Ransom said.

"Yeah," Noah said. "I was supposed to have been at Jack's place the night Archimedes killed him," he said finally. "If I'd been there, Jack might still be alive."

A gasp sounded behind him. Noah whirled around. Lyssa's stunned expression twisted his heart.

"Lyssa—"

She backed away from him, shaking her head. "No. Just…I can't believe this."

"Get me that plane," Noah said and ended the call.

He stuffed the phone into his pocket. Lyssa turned and rushed into the sleet. The cold ice soaked her hair. Noah grabbed her and pulled her back into the hangar. He pushed her bangs away from her face. "Lyssa, I…"

She looked up into his eyes, the emerald depths filled with pain. "Why didn't you tell me?"

"What was I supposed to say?" He'd been dreading this moment for two years. For two years he'd lived with the regret.

"If you'd been there…" Her voice cracked.

"I could have saved him."

Lyssa's knees gave way. Noah propped her up against him. She struggled to breathe. "You and Jack could have taken him. None of this would be happening. I'd have—"

"You'd have your life back," Noah finished, a whisper in her ear. "You'd have Jack. I wish I'd been there for you," he said. "Jack and I, we *would* have stopped him."

She clutched the collar of his coat. "That's why you're really helping me, isn't it? Not because you and Jack were best friends, but because you were supposed to be there that night."

"Partly," Noah said. "I owe Jack my life. You know that." He tilted her chin up to search her eyes. "But make no mistake, Lyssa, I'm here for you."

A small flush rose in her cheeks. Her lips parted. Her gaze heated.

Noah tensed. His entire being urged him to kiss her, to comfort her, to remind her that he would always be here for her.

She didn't give him a chance.

"Thank you," she said and pulled his head down to hers.

Stunned, he let her kiss him. Her lips parted and she swept her tongue inside his mouth.

With a groan, a wave of longing rushed through him. He pulled her close and captured her lips, drinking in the sweetness.

He lifted his head, stunned at the emotions sparking between them. She blinked up at him, her own expression frozen.

"I didn't expect—" she whispered.

He touched her swollen lips with his thumb. "Me neither. You're more than I ever imagined."

A loud throat-clearing interrupted them. "Noah, we need you out here," Rafe called from the hangar's entrance.

Noah didn't move away from her. He didn't want to leave the warm softness pressing against him. "In a minute."

His hand trembled as he touched Lyssa's face. These

feelings terrified him. Long buried dreams resurfaced. Desires he'd denied because of his friendship with Jack.

She gripped his hands and pulled them away from her. "This isn't right," she whispered softly. "I shouldn't have—"

"Don't say it." He couldn't bear her regret. Part of him knew he was just second best, just a substitute for Jack. For her true love.

She took a shuddering breath. "You don't understand. There are things you don't know."

"Secrets. I know."

Her eyes widened. "No. Oh, no, you can't know. No one knows."

"Reid knew."

She backed away, the cold air rushing between them. "You're trying to goad me. There are things I won't talk about, Noah. I can't."

Her words gutted him. "You have to trust me, Lyssa."

"Everyone I ever trusted is dead...or in a coma. I won't do that to you. Or to me."

Back stiff, Lyssa walked out of the hangar into the weather. Noah followed, ignoring the curious expressions on Rafe's and Zane's faces.

The back door of the SUV had lifted into place, protecting them from the sleet. Zane held a receiver in his hand and he ran it slowly over the bags in the back of the SUV. One by one, he placed them into the vehicle.

"Anything?" Noah asked, his voice raised over the thwack of ice on the car. They had to figure out how Archimedes knew where they were.

"I ramped up the signal, but nothing yet." Zane scowled. "He shouldn't have found us here. I don't get it. Maybe you can figure it out."

"What about my ready bag," Lyssa said and moved closer to Zane. "I kept it in the closet."

"I went over everything," Zane said. "Even your weapons. Nice, by the way."

A loud beeping sounded from the machine. "What the hell?"

He shifted it, and the beeping got more high-pitched as he brought it toward Lyssa.

She backed away.

"Stay still," Zane said.

He moved the machine up and down the length of Lyssa's body. It stopped just at the top curve of her breasts. Zane flushed a bit. "Um…have you got anything…"

Noah tugged at the gold chain around her neck. Her engagement ring.

Zane held the monitor close to it. A piercing tone erupted.

He looked up at Lyssa. She stared down at the diamond.

"It's your ring." Noah said. "Jack's ring brought Archimedes here."

Chapter Eight

The thin air of Denver made it hard to breathe. Archimedes took out his inhaler and wrapped his lips around the mouthpiece for a puff. Within seconds, the invisible clamp around his lungs eased. He glared at the medicine before pocketing it. He hated the telltale weakness. One more reason the kids at school had teased him, made him the fool.

Didn't matter he'd earned a perfect score on the SAT in math. Or that he'd been accepted to MIT. He still wound up dumped in the garbage bin behind the school. And with his clothes stolen out of his gym-class locker.

The world preyed on the weak. It's why he'd become strong.

He *would* have respect. He'd earned it.

The luxury rental car purred and the warmth of the heater circulated around him. He opened his laptop and connected to the internet via a secure satellite connection. A few quick taps on the keyboard and the search result for "Bradford" appeared.

Fools. He hadn't even had to work for the information.

Five addresses. Paul, Sierra, Mitch and Emily, Chase and Noah.

Archimedes knew exactly where Noah Bradford was. He glanced at the small screen. A red dot blinked at an airport in Texas.

He imagined the uncertainty, and the fear. Archimedes smiled. They had to be wondering when and where the next surprise would hit them.

Soon. Very soon.

Archimedes had left enough clues to know where they were heading next. Exactly where he wanted them to go.

Alessandra had the means to get to Connecticut.

Everything was proceeding precisely as planned.

With one exception.

Archimedes flicked the screen and stared at the still from the video from Lyssa's apartment. He studied Alessandra's hand clinging to Noah's. Archimedes zoomed once more onto her face.

She wanted Noah.

He wanted her.

Archimedes tossed the offending image away. He had to get that man away from Alessandra. Noah Bradford needed to be taught a lesson, and Archimedes knew exactly how.

A few more taps at the computer and he hit the enter key. The executable file did its job. Within minutes, five feeds from traffic cameras displayed on his screen. Live shots in front of the five Bradford residences.

Now all Archimedes had to do was wait.

As if the heavens heard Lyssa's cry, they opened up and small bits of hail pinged off the metal of the SUV. Her devastation tore at Noah's heart.

She gripped his wet hands and tugged her necklace out of his grasp. "It's not possible. He can't be using my ring to find us."

Knowing what he asked of her, Noah simply held out his hand. "I need it, Lyssa."

For a moment he wondered if she'd refuse him. Finally,

reluctantly, she lifted the chain over her head and handed it to him.

"Let's get out of this weather," he said.

Zane and Rafe followed as they all raced into the hangar, the hangar where she'd kissed Noah, where she'd clung to him. Now she looked at him if she wished he would disappear. Noah slammed the door closed behind them. Wet and cold, she wrapped her arms around her shivering body, not once leaning into him for comfort.

Not that he'd expected her to.

Not that he'd hoped she would.

Liar.

Noah gave the ring to Zane. The techie pulled a small magnifying glass from his bag. He studied the diamond then handed the magnifier to Noah. "Take a look."

Noah peered through the glass. Archimedes was damn brilliant.

Lyssa clutched his arm. "What is it?"

"A microtransmitter attached to the diamond. He definitely used the ring to track you."

His fingers held the ring that Jack had presented to Lyssa—a piece of jewelry Lyssa clearly still cherished.

"But…it was hidden in the jewelry box. How could Archimedes know I would take it?"

"He knows you love Jack."

It hurt Noah to say the words. Even though they were true. All he had to do was look at Lyssa to recognize the truth of her feelings.

"We have to get rid of the ring, Lyssa," Zane said. "Or he'll follow us."

"No! That ring is important. I can't give it up." Lyssa grabbed the jewelry from Noah, holding it close to her heart. "Please. Find a way for me to keep it."

Noah winced at her desperate longing. He glanced at Zane. "We can remove the chip without damaging the ring."

A smile tilted the corner of Zane's mouth. "I like your devious mind, Falcon. Use it as bait. Yep, I love the idea of putting one over on this guy for a change." He crossed the room and created a makeshift workbench out of several crates.

Noah pulled out a chair for Lyssa. "This could take a while. And with this weather, we're not going anywhere."

"I'll take first watch," Rafe said quietly, pulling his hood over his head and stepping out into the weather.

Noah grabbed a small space heater from the corner of the hangar and set it up near Lyssa.

The fan blew warm air toward her. She rubbed her hands and slipped out of her soggy coat, draping it over a wooden crate. Noah did the same before crouching next to her. For a few moments he'd wondered if there was a chance for them…but he should have known better.

He could never live up to Jack's memory; he would never earn her trust. He might understand that, but he didn't like it.

When the blue tinge of her lips turned pink and her teeth stopped chattering, she looked up at him. "Falcon?" Lyssa's brow arched.

Noah shrugged. "A name I'm known by. You should probably forget it." Hopefully she would. The Falcon had a price on his head. He'd saved a lot of lives, but he'd taken more than his share.

Zane let out a small curse across the room. "I could use another set of hands, Falcon. You're the integrated-circuit wizard."

"Be right there." Noah checked the time. "CTC's plane should be here as soon as the weather breaks, Lyssa. We'll get to Connecticut. We'll find him. Your ring may give us the break we need."

He rose and started to the back of the hangar.

"Noah."

Lyssa's soft voice made him pause. He looked over his shoulder.

"Thank you. For saving the ring. It's more important to me than you can imagine."

The words made Noah's heart ache. "I know, Lyssa. I know."

LYSSA DIDN'T KNOW how many times she wanted to cross the hangar to Noah. He huddled with Zane, each wielding tiny screwdrivers and focused expressions. She'd hurt him. She knew it.

But what could she say? Better to leave them be. She couldn't tell Noah why the ring was so important. That she wanted her daughter to have a little piece of her father, wanted her little girl to know how much Jack would have loved her.

She couldn't give that truth away. For his sake as much as her own.

The slam of the metal door caused her to reach for her weapon until she recognized Rafe's soaking figure stomping into the hangar.

The heater had warmed up the place, at least until Rafe had opened the outside door. Lyssa rubbed her arms to ward off the cold gust of wind. The storm had worsened. No way would an aircraft be taking off anytime soon.

They were stuck in Dallas.

"If Archimedes is still here, he's invisible," Rafe said, brushing ice from his coat and hair. He walked straight over and warmed his hands by the heater. "It's bad out there."

"Well, we've caught a break," Noah stood, joining them,

an envelope in one hand, her necklace in the other. Zane sauntered behind Noah. He raised the small paper. "The microdot. Safe, sound, and intact."

Zane snagged the tracer from his bag, placing it next to the ring first. Nothing sounded. He tested the envelope. The device squealed.

Noah smiled, though the light didn't reach his eyes. "Archimedes will follow this." He pried open a wooden crate, placed the envelope inside, then nailed it shut. "For now, he'll think we're still at the airport."

"We're not staying here?" Lyssa asked.

"The weather isn't clearing. CTC's plane can't land. We can't get out, but Archimedes can't trace us, either. It's time we reclaimed our advantage."

Noah didn't meet her gaze. He'd turned all business, their connection severed.

Maybe it was for the best.

Within minutes they'd gathered up their things. Lyssa raced to the SUV, snow, sleet and rain in a combination that had her slipping the last few feet. She nearly fell, but Noah scooped her into his arms and placed her in the backseat. Once she was settled, he turned to her and held out his hand.

The gold chain dropped and the sparkling ring swung from the necklace.

Her heart sped up. She clasped it to her. The ring was all she had of Jack. All Jocelyn would ever have.

"Thank you." She swallowed around the thickness of her voice. "It means the world to me."

Noah gave her a sharp nod and then readied his weapon, staring into the dim light of the afternoon storm. It's not that she didn't trust Noah to keep her secret if he could. But she didn't trust that Archimedes wouldn't win.

Noah probably wouldn't understand the distinction.

By the time Rafe pulled into the front of a hotel near the airport and slipped out to check them in, Lyssa couldn't handle the quiet any longer. "Noah—"

"Weather report says we'll have to wait for at least several hours," he interrupted, his tone curt. "Maybe longer."

A small sigh escaped from her. She was doing the right thing, wasn't she? What if she told him? Lyssa knew exactly what would happen. Noah would want to know where Jocelyn was. He'd want to protect the baby.

While Lyssa would do anything to hold her daughter in her arms, she'd become a pragmatist. She'd made a choice. Her daughter's life over her own.

For now, Jocelyn was safe. If Lyssa tried to get in touch with them… A shudder settled at the base of her spine. Archimedes would find out.

Rafe opened the front door of the SUV and slid inside. "I got us a suite." He grinned at Noah. "You paid."

"I'm assuming you didn't use my credit card?"

"Nah," Zane said. "I transferred your money to our new fearless leader. Ned Bourne. Jason's younger brother." He chuckled.

At Noah's slow shake of his head, Lyssa bit back a small smile.

The engine roared to life and Rafe pulled around to the back entrance of the hotel. "We'll drop you off then pick up food. No reason to make ourselves visible," Rafe said.

He tossed Noah the key. Noah snagged it from the air then grabbed a laptop from the backseat. Lyssa shouldered her duffel and followed him into the hallway.

They rode the elevator in silence. When they reached the door, Noah stretched his arm in front of her body. He checked out the room, nodded, and allowed her to go in. He said nothing, but emptied his computer case and set up his laptop on the table in the suite's sitting area, attaching a small black box to the internet cable.

"What's that?"

"I don't want anyone tracing my signal," he said. "Zane may think he's the computer whiz around CTC, but I hold my own." He gave her a long look. "I know what I'm doing, Lyssa."

Lyssa hovered for a moment before taking a breath of courage and sitting beside him. How could she apologize without explaining? "Jack told me you were more than good. He called you a genius."

Noah tapped the keys, his face stoic. Finally he leaned back in his chair. "What are you doing?"

"I'm trying to apologize," Lyssa said. "You *could* make it easy on me."

Noah twisted in his chair, facing her. "You made a choice not to trust me, Lyssa. I thought we'd come further than that. My mistake." He turned to his computer and started typing. "We'll keep our relationship just business. It's probably best anyway. No small talk necessary."

His fingers tapped away at the keyboard. She didn't move. She sneaked a few glances at the strong line of his jaw, the intense focus.

This wasn't right. He was Jack's best friend. She placed her hand on Noah's arm. "Um…Jack said you owned more than one company when you went into basic training together?"

His hands stilled and his gaze rose from the monitor. "This isn't necessary."

"Yes, it is. You're doing everything you can to help me," she said. "I don't like the strain between us."

"Strain?" He rose and bent over her chair, his hands on each armrest. His big body loomed large, his hooded gaze dangerous—not to her safety but to her sanity.

"You think learning more about me will make me forget that you haven't been honest? You think a few words will make the tension between us go away? What's happening between us is about way more than trust, Lyssa, and you know it."

His breath warmed her cheek, his lips nearly touching her as they hovered just above her skin. She swallowed, the gulp seeming to echo in the room.

"I see you get the message." He pulled away slightly. "You have a choice to make, and one road leads to you going all in."

The words sent a shiver to her core, not of fear, but of longing. She placed her hand on his chest. His heart thudded against her palm.

A knock sounded at the door, the pattern of the taps obviously preplanned.

Noah cleared his throat. "Rafe and Zane."

Slipping his gun from his pants, he peered through the keyhole. He turned back. "You're starting on a dangerous path," he whispered. "Be very sure it's what you want."

He opened the door. The scent of mesquite-smoked barbecue filled the room. While Rafe and Zane set up a huge meal, Lyssa couldn't stop staring at Noah. He was right. She had a choice to make.

Archimedes might be dangerous to her life, but Noah Bradford brought a whole new kind of danger—and if she let her heart rule her head, she'd never be the same.

THE BRADFORDS MADE everything difficult. Archimedes clutched the laptop, squeezing the frustration building from deep within. Hours had passed. All of the family homes were empty; completely deserted.

Perhaps he could create a reason for Noah's family to come home.

He clicked on the image outside of Noah Bradford's driveway entrance. He zoomed in. Security. And not just any security—security from Bradford's Dreamcatcher company. It would be much easier to leave a message at one of the other houses, but Archimedes liked a challenge. He'd always thrived on a mental battle.

He always won.

All he had to do was jam the signal. He entered the coordinates of Noah Bradford's house into his computer. Before he could execute the file, an image moved across his screen.

He paused.

A bright yellow Jeep pulled into Noah Bradford's driveway. An arm reached out and keyed in a password. The light brown hair that stuck out reminded him of Lyssa. Quickly, he glanced at the tracker. The blinking dot in Dallas, Texas, quieted his pounding pulse. She was still at the airport.

So who was this woman?

He opened his file and studied the only woman in the group. Not as beautiful as Alessandra. Sierra Bradford. Her jaw too strong; her eyes too knowing. He didn't like her.

Still, she was a gift.

The vehicle drove through the gate. He quickly typed in a few codes. Encrypted. He couldn't commandeer the signal, but he was only fifteen minutes away.

He made it in twelve. She hadn't come out yet.

Slipping on his latex gloves, Archimedes rounded his trunk. Digging into the back of his bag, he filled a dart with liquid and loaded the weapon. He got into the driver's seat and waited.

Five minutes passed, then ten. He could be patient. Eventually she would come out.

Another eight minutes went by before the gate slid open.

Archimedes shoved the gear into Drive, his hand patting the gun. He maneuvered the vehicle to the side so he'd have a clear view.

She opened her window to close the gate.

He shot the dart.

Sierra Bradford slumped over the steering wheel.

Archimedes smiled.

Noah Bradford would be very sorry he'd ever tried to steal Alessandra.

WIND BUFFETED THE panes of the hotel room windows. Lyssa shivered at the cold seeping through the flimsy glass panes. She could tell the temperature had dropped at least another ten degrees since they'd holed up in the hotel.

Noah stood in the corner, his cell phone to his ear. "Just get here as soon as you can." He turned to Lyssa, a frown on his face. "The plane won't make it here until morning." He tossed the phone on the bed and opened the blinds. "On the positive side, if we can't travel, neither can Archimedes."

Rafe stroked his beard. "Better not take any chances. We know he was here. Zane and I will stake out the hangar. Maybe we'll get lucky."

Lyssa jumped up from the table. "Not alone."

Zane simply winked at her. "That's what you're paying us for, sweetheart."

Before she could think of an argument, the two men left. A knot lodged in Lyssa's stomach. "What if Archimedes follows the signal? He won't hesitate to kill them."

"Rafe and Zane know what they're doing," Noah said. "They've faced terrorists and guerrilla warriors. They're smart, savvy and they know how to stay alive."

"Archimedes is smarter. And he doesn't make mistakes," she said flatly. She picked up her duffel. "I'm going with them."

Noah grabbed the strap and whirled her away from the door. "Like hell you are."

She righted herself and yanked her bag to her. "Don't you see what's happening, Noah? He's playing us. He'll win. It's inevitable." She kneaded the base of her neck. "Maybe it's better if he *does* win. If he kills me, then it will be over."

Noah clasped her shoulders. "Don't delude yourself. He'll go on killing. He's developed a taste for it. He'll just turn his fixation onto someone else."

Oh, God. Lyssa's fingers loosened and the bag fell between them. She bowed her head, her forehead hitting his chest. "You're right. How can I be so selfish?"

Warm arms surrounded her. "You're exhausted. You have a serial killer after you. You're entitled."

Noah pressed her closer against him. She didn't resist. She'd made her choice. She didn't know how long she'd survive, but she couldn't resist the temptation any longer. She wrapped her arms around Noah's waist, just wanting to be close, just wanting to forget that there was a madman who wanted her dead. He tilted her chin and looked down at her, his brown eyes intense. She squirmed under that knowing look.

"Are you sure?" he asked quietly.

She couldn't look away. Her gaze drifted to the tension in his jaw. He swallowed and she focused on his eyes. They'd gone dark, the color of mahogany. He stood so close she could feel his heart beating. Her leg touched his; her chest rested against the hard planes of his body. She could anticipate each breath he took.

He stroked her cheek. "I want to kiss you again." His

head lowered so slowly, the anticipation sent a tingle through her lips. "You can stop me with one word," he whispered.

She pulled his head down to hers, her mouth opening under his lips. "Make me forget, Noah. For just a little while."

A groan escaped from his throat. He tightened his hold, lifting her by the hips. She wrapped her legs around his waist and he backed toward the hotel bed.

He tasted of spice and coffee and something indefinably Noah. She gripped his shoulders and held on, sinking to the bed. She straddled his hips and held his head between her hands.

Her mouth pressed against his. She hadn't been touched in so long; she'd been running, at Archimedes's whim, for what seemed like forever.

Well, he wasn't here. Not now.

Noah leaned back, taking her with him. She pressed his wrists back against the bed, stretching his arms above his head.

He let her.

She could tell he wanted her. He couldn't hide his response. She ground her hips against his hardness. So tempting.

"You're close to the point of no return," he gasped, his hips arching to her.

She leaned over him and took his lips.

A ring sounded from his pocket. She sagged against him, her breath short. He let out a harsh curse and she moved her hands from his wrists, shoving back the disappointment. She tried to climb off him. He held her waist, holding her in place with one hand.

She could have moved but she didn't.

When he fished out his phone from his front pocket, he

moaned a bit. "I'm going to kill whoever interrupted you. Don't lose your place."

She wiggled against him and he surged beneath her.

"Bradford. This better be good."

Noah's brow narrowed, his expression grew fierce. Lyssa stiffened above him and leaned closer so she could hear the conversation on the other end. Noah looked as if he wanted to move away, keep her from listening. That was *so* not happening.

She snuggled closer, and he bit back a groan.

"All the forensic evidence collected for the Archimedes murders has been destroyed." Elijah's voice filtered through the earpiece. "From a legal standpoint, we're starting from scratch."

Immediately Lyssa rolled off Noah. So, a trial wouldn't be possible. It gave them only one choice, and part of her was relieved. Noah's arm snaked around her and tugged her against him. She relaxed and let him anchor her close.

"How did Archimedes get to it?" Noah asked.

"Oh, he made it look like an accident—if you believe in oceanfront property in Arizona. A kerosene lamp just above the Archimedes evidence section. A wire short circuit. A fire. A convenient computer virus. Panic is racing through the Justice Department."

"Find the leak, Elijah." Noah's gaze held her captive. "It doesn't change what we have to do, but it may give us a lead on Archimedes's identity."

Noah's finger trailed a soft stroke down her arm. Her body shivered under his touch, but her mind pulled away. Every moment she was with Noah, the wall around her heart splintered a bit more. She was a fool.

Noah ended the call with orders for Elijah to keep in contact. Lyssa placed her hands on Noah's chest and pushed at him. "Let me go," she said.

He rolled her under him, holding his weight up on his forearm. "It's a blow to the prosecution," Noah admitted. "But it doesn't change our plans. In some ways it's what you wanted, isn't it?"

As if he could read her mind.

She couldn't meet his gaze. "He would never have been convicted anyway. Reasonable doubt."

The warmth of his body didn't budge, but she shifted in his arms, staring at the wall. "Promise me something," she said softly. "Promise me he won't go free. Promise me, if something happens and I can't do it…promise me Archimedes won't walk away. No court. No trial."

He stayed silent for what seemed like hours, but it may have been only a few seconds. "I promise," he said finally.

Lyssa pushed at his shoulders. He let her and eased off her body. She rose from the bed, then looked at him over her shoulder. "Thank you."

She paced the room. He sat up on the edge of the bed and reached out a hand, capturing hers. "I want a promise from you." He drew her near. "Don't take him on by yourself. Let me do this."

With a sharp yank, she pulled away, shaking her head. "I…I can't, Noah. I vowed to Jack. It's my battle."

Noah's eyes bored into her. "Have you ever killed a man?" he asked.

"I watched the man I love die. I saw a WitSec officer assigned to protect me carved up on my apartment floor. I watched an innocent woman stop breathing and a man I respected with his throat cut," she said harshly. "I'm way too familiar with death."

"Taking a life changes you, Lyssa. It's something you can't ever take back." He cupped her face in his hands. "Let me do this for you."

Lyssa tugged at the ring around her neck. She lifted her gaze to his. "I'd give up my soul to see Archimedes dead."

He kissed her palm. "Not by these hands. I promise you that."

DARKNESS HAD FALLEN over the Rocky Mountains. Archimedes flicked the small but bright flashlight on in the abandoned building. He dragged Sierra Bradford into a small closet at the center of the structure and propped her up against the back wall. Outside, sirens wailed, but no one would find them here. He'd made certain.

His chest wheezed with each breath through the stocking mask. He'd be glad to return to the coast. Bending down, he tested the climbing cords securing her hands and feet. The knots wouldn't give; they were strong and nearly indestructible.

Last, he pressed duct tape to her mouth, leaving her free to breathe through her nose.

He wouldn't kill her. Not yet. Partly because he wanted Bradford to believe there was a chance his sister could be saved.

More importantly, he wanted his victim to know what was happening every hour she waited. He relished the fear, had come to savor those moments when eyes widened with terror, then resignation, then finally the flicker of life snuffing out.

He had total, absolute control over all existence.

So, he waited, and watched, until her eyelids fluttered a bit.

He smiled, crouching down in front of her so he would be the first thing she'd see.

Her eyelids snapped open.

He could tell the moment she recognized her position. She twisted, but the tight fit of the closet stopped her.

"Don't bother trying to escape."

The flashlight swept down her body.

Archimedes waited for the panic to settle in her eyes. Instead, her expression skewered him with hatred.

His temple throbbed.

Fool.

"Do you know who I am?" he asked, his voice a sing-song whisper.

She simply glared. No response. Not even a shake of her head.

His teeth ground. She couldn't ignore him. He wouldn't allow it.

He lifted his knee and slammed the steel-toe boots against her ribs. She folded up, whimpering through the duct tape.

"Do you know me?" he asked.

No response.

He kicked her again. "Do you know me? Answer me!"

She shook her head, just barely.

He grinned, hoping his distorted face through the stocking terrified her. "Allow me to introduce myself. I am Archimedes."

This time her eyes did widen and he got what he wanted. A flash of fear.

Satisfaction gave way to power. His grin widened. "I see you know me. You should."

He leaned forward, his hands moving closer. Her gaze followed them. He toyed with the buttons on her manly shirt. She shrank back, but she couldn't escape. He liked playing with her. The woman who pretended she was so capable, so strong.

She was nothing.

He unbuttoned the top button, staring at the smooth,

unblemished skin, then pulled out a knife. "Don't worry. This won't take long."

Suddenly the woman kicked out at him, her heel hitting just above his knee. He fell to the side, then sprang toward her, sitting on her legs.

He pressed the knife against her throat. "Do that again, you're dead."

Enough playing around. With a few quick slices, he cut through her shirt and bra, baring her chest.

He dug the knife into her smooth skin, carving his symbol at the top of her breast.

She winced, but didn't cry out. Damn her.

"Are you afraid?" He dragged the blade to her rib. "One shove in right here and you'd bleed to death on the inside." He moved the blade to her abdomen. "Or here, it would take longer."

He gloried at the shiver that raced through her before finishing the design. "Or not."

Blood dripped down to her nipple. He gazed at his handiwork.

Infinity. Forever.

How long he'd loved Alessandra. How long they would be together.

How much longer before she would be his?

It had to be soon.

He tapped his temple. "I should kill you, but I need you alive. For a while." He rose, wiping his blade clean. "In thirty-six hours this building will be demolished. If your brother does what he's told, I might let him know where you are before the explosions commence. Otherwise…"

Archimedes exited the closet and fortified the door. She would die soon. And Noah Bradford would learn once and for all what it meant to challenge Archimedes.

They all would learn.

Chapter Nine

Noah took the night watch from a spot on the wall with a view of both the suite door and the outside window. Rafe and Zane had done their share of staking out already in freezing temperatures. Archimedes hadn't shown and they deserved the rest.

Besides, Noah knew he wouldn't sleep. Whenever he closed his eyes, Lyssa's sweet voice seduced him. In the dreams, she started out wanting him, begging for his touch, and then ended by presenting him a bloody knife—to kill for her.

He didn't need a psychology degree to comprehend the meaning.

Did she want him…or did she want the Falcon? Killing the ones who believed they could get away with it.

Archimedes fit the category.

So did most of the terrorist leaders he'd tracked down and eliminated.

The soft swish of Lyssa's bedroom door took Noah out of his thoughts. He glanced at the red numbers of the radio clock on the end table in the sitting area. Four in the morning.

Lyssa padded across the room and sank down beside him, tucking her knees and wrapping her arms around her legs.

"You're up early," he said, his voice husky from a night without speaking to anyone, except in his mind.

"I never went to sleep," she said softly. "Still snowing?"

"Light. We'll be able to leave as soon as they clear the runways. I would think midmorning."

She rested her chin on her knees and looked over at him. "I've been thinking about you. About us."

Oh, boy. Noah wasn't sure he wanted to hear this. "Your conclusion?" Did he even want to know?

"You confuse me," she said, chewing on her lip. "Jack couldn't quite figure you out. He told me…"

Noah waited for the teasing, the mocking. Jack had respected Noah's ability, he knew that, but Jack hadn't been able to resist a jibe or two about the human calculator.

"Your smarts blew him away. He didn't talk about work a lot, but he couldn't help but mention a few crazy Mac-Gyver stunts you'd pulled off. One with toothpicks, duct tape and some blasting caps."

"That mission was classified," Noah said. He leaned back against the wall. "Jack was convinced I'd gone nuts for coming to boot camp, especially when he found out about Dreamcatcher."

She smiled, her expression bittersweet, and Noah couldn't stop himself from being caught in the sad depths of her green eyes.

"He couldn't understand why someone with your brains and your money would be willing to fight so hard to be a marine. Mostly because Jack's father had told him it was either the military or working in his dad's auto-body shop."

"I'd forgotten that story," Noah said with a slight grin. "The truth is, Jack was made for Intelligence. His charm got him information I could never have gathered. Plus he had guts. He was loyal, and he could sniff out the bad guys like he was a bloodhound. Great instincts."

"He said the same about you, but he said you did it with your brain and techie toys." She tilted her head to the side. "Why did you join up? Why not just run your companies?"

He shrugged, bending his leg at the knee, studying the light dusting of snow still falling. "I was good at school. I tinkered a lot with computers and stuff. Not much of an athlete."

She poked at his biceps. "No way."

"Believe me. I was the kid that got called egghead. My dad was a cop, my brothers kick-butt athletes. My sister... well, Sierra is a math whiz and a state-champion volleyball player. And then there was me. The brain. Uncoordinated, skinny. A computer geek."

"I would never have guessed."

"I was an enigma to my family, stayed in the basement playing with a computer my dad bought me for Christmas when that's all I begged for. Then, in high school I got into encryption and decryption. I developed a couple of decryption programs. My math teacher talked to Dad. They got the patents. The companies were born. My career was set."

"So, why did you enlist?"

Noah chuckled. "Man, you should have seen my dad's face when I told him. I thought he was going to faint."

"I'll bet. The brains of the family choosing the Marines." Her gaze bored into his very being. "You didn't want to be who you were. You wanted to be more like the rest of your family. You wanted to fit in."

Noah stilled. He said nothing. How could she know?

"You wear your masks well. Both of them. The Falcon and Noah Bradford, genius and CEO. But who's Noah, the man?" Lyssa leaned closer, placing her hand on his leg.

He tensed under her touch, unable to move away.

"Not very many people look beneath the surface, do they?"

"Why are you? Why now?"

"Because lying alone in that bed I realized something. I've worked for two years to perfect my own mask. I hate that not one person I've met in the last two years really knows me. It's lonely. Do you find it lonely, Noah?"

His body leaned toward her, almost as if a string tugged them ever closer. He could practically feel the heat of her body, and his own responded, surging to life, tempted beyond reason.

"I remembered what Jack said about you," she whispered. "I compared his stories to what I've witnessed the last three days. I finally understood what's been bothering me. You're not who I expected when Reid said he'd be sending you."

Noah sent her a wary look. "Is that good or bad?"

"Both. I thought you'd be a killing machine."

Noah winced. She wasn't wrong.

She clutched his hand, squeezing it hard. "Don't pull away. I realize now Reid sent the Falcon. Someone who would help me and then disappear from my life." She leaned into him. "That's who I met our first few minutes together, but you're more than the Falcon. You care. About me, about Jack, about the other victims. That, Noah Bradford, is my problem." She took a deep breath. "Because tonight I realized I could fall in love with the man you hide behind the mask."

His heart thudded in response to her words. He'd given away too much. He'd let those long-ago dreams of her distract him.

To save her, he needed to be the Falcon. Not Noah.

Noah had to stay buried, even if it meant losing Lyssa.

The buzzing of his phone saved him. He stood, needing to get away from Lyssa's overwhelming presence.

Rafe and Zane appeared in the doorway, alert.

"Bradford."

"It's Ransom. Rich will have the plane at the airport around nine in the morning. Be ready."

"We leave the hotel no later than seven," Noah said. He looked at Lyssa. "Try to get some sleep. We'll wake you in a couple of hours."

"Don't do this, Noah," Lyssa pleaded.

"Call me Falcon."

CTC's PLANE ARRIVED on time.

Snow blanketed the area around the small airport. The flurries had finally stopped, and the runway had been cleared. Noah climbed the plane's stairs, the wind whipping through his coat. The chill went straight through to his soul. Lyssa hadn't said two words to him since she'd walked to her bedroom, head held high.

The pilot, Rich, offered Noah the captain's chair.

"Not enough sleep last night," he said. Rich nodded and headed out to do the final preflight check.

Noah moved into the cabin.

Lyssa had taken a seat next to Rafe. His friend lifted an eyebrow as Noah buckled in across from them.

Noah wanted to kill Archimedes. Slowly and painfully. Mostly because the guy deserved it for every life he'd taken. Noah forced himself not to look into Lyssa's eyes. She'd reminded him of something important. Of how much he had to lose if he let his emotions take over. He'd been there and done that. The results had been disastrous.

"Do you have Archimedes's tracking chip?" Noah asked Zane.

"Sure thing, Falcon." Zane showed him the envelope. "Working perfectly."

Lyssa gripped her armrests, her knuckles whitening. "He's tracking us right now?"

"That's the point," Noah said. "If we block the signal—you have figured out how to do that, right?"

Zane shook his head. "Sorry. If I disrupt the signal, he'll know we know about it."

Noah scowled. "We'll work with it." He looked at Lyssa. "We *want* him to find us…but on our terms. Not his."

"What's your plan?"

"We set a trap. Somewhere he won't be able to resist revisiting. Somewhere he missed out on the prize of a lifetime."

Lyssa's complexion lost all its color.

Noah wanted nothing more than to take her in his arms, but he couldn't. He shoved aside the instinct. The Falcon didn't hold his clients, he protected them. "That's right. We're going to Jack's house."

BY THE TIME the plane landed in New York and they'd traveled to Darien, Connecticut, Lyssa knew the afternoon sun wouldn't be shining much longer. Noah dropped Zane off a few hundred yards to the north of Jack's house then pulled the SUV off on a dirt road to the south.

Despite the fact that Rafe had the chip and was heading toward the UN building, Lyssa still couldn't drive away the feeling of foreboding. Her pulse fluttering, she exited the vehicle, hand on her weapon. Noah palmed his Glock and they made their way toward the home she'd shared with Jack.

Shadows climbed up the sides of the abandoned house nestled in the small wooden glade. Jack had picked it for several reasons: one was defense. The other was the backyard. Where they'd wanted their children to play.

The dream that Archimedes destroyed.

Noah stopped Lyssa with one hand. He signaled for her to wait.

Archimedes knew they would be here eventually. Still, part of her hoped he'd be here now. She wanted this over. Whatever happened, at least it would be done.

She could go with Noah's plan. Set the trap. Hide, then Rafe would bring the tracking chip, and they would wait Archimedes out.

Except the serial killer seemed to read minds.

She could tell Noah wasn't used to anyone being able to get the better of him. His forefinger scratched the knuckle of his thumb rhythmically. She'd noticed it more than once. In fact, the more frustrated he became, the more the small tell gave away his emotions.

They crept closer to the house, Zane to the north, keeping watch.

Lyssa's entire body froze as they entered the backyard. She couldn't stop herself. Her nerves were shot. She gripped Noah's arm, her hold tight.

This was the first time she'd returned to their home since Jack's death. Law enforcement had packed her bags, and when they'd recognized she might be the only person left alive to identify Archimedes, they'd whisked her away. Not that it had done any good.

Silently, Noah opened a bag and pulled out a crowbar. He pried off several boards at the rear of the house, the creaking echoing through the night.

He tossed the boards onto the dead grass. With a sidelong glance, he studied her. "You okay?"

With the words, Noah touched her arm. His strength calmed her a bit. If being here would get them Archimedes, then she wouldn't let a little thing like fear stand in her way.

She nodded, but it was a lie. She didn't want to go inside. The memories were so very good and so very bad. This was the place where she and Jack had loved, laughed, made love. Where he'd proposed to her, kissed her, held her. Made a baby.

And where he'd died saving her life.

Noah jimmied the last board away from the door. She placed her hand on the jamb and closed her eyes. She could do this.

He knelt beside her and with two long prongs picked the lock in seconds, then grabbed an electronic device from his bag of tricks. He ran the scanner around the wood. "Clear."

Cautiously he pressed the screen and the door swung open, creaking, revealing a darkened room inside.

Lyssa took a deep breath as Noah stepped across the threshold, part of her waiting for another Archimedes surprise.

Nothing happened.

That didn't diminish the knot of tension spreading through her shoulders.

Noah snapped on his flashlight. The beam swept across the kitchen. With each new illuminated section of tile, her heart hitched.

No one had done a thing since the cops had searched the place. The light bounced off the dust gathering on the oak table, its thickness obscuring the grain of the wood.

"Anything strike you as unusual?" Noah asked as they walked through the chaos.

"Besides the fact that cops make lousy housekeepers?" she said, trying to maintain control.

"Better than my place," Noah said. He squeezed her arm. "You're doing great."

"A lot you know."

Lyssa stopped in the center of the kitchen. The cabinet above the refrigerator was the only one unopened.

Could it still be there?

Ignoring Noah, she climbed onto the round step stool that Jack had placed in the corner of the kitchen for her.

"What are you looking for?" Noah asked.

"Nothing, just seeing if they missed anything," she lied.

She peered inside, moved the cookie jar out of the way and let out a small sigh. Except for Reid, her secret remained safe. In her vision lay a silver rattle and a pair of baby shoes.

THE SCENT OF peanut sauce floated through the front door of the restaurant. This was Rose's favorite place, but Archimedes hated coming here. He longed to be in his germ-free apartment, watching the video, waiting for Lyssa to arrive. Waiting for her to understand the final clues to his message.

She *would* prove her worth. She had to. He wouldn't consider any alternative.

Lyssa would come to him.

Unable to resist, Archimedes glanced at the blinking light on the small screen of his phone. Fools. The tracking device showed them moving toward the United Nations. Following the trail of the insipid Frederick Allen.

Why couldn't Lyssa see where she should be going?

Eventually, she'd have to return to where the journey began. But that time, she'd be on her own. Noah Bradford would be dealt with soon.

Then Lyssa would be his and his alone.

Archimedes pocketed the device and walked into the small café. He catalogued the floor. Clean. He weaved through the chairs, making certain he didn't touch anything on his way to Rose.

She sat at their usual corner table, staring down at the tablecloth. Demure, controllable.

Just as he preferred.

Her chin rose and his step faltered. Gone was the typical smile of welcome. She frowned at him, a vertical wrinkle creasing her forehead.

When he reached her, she jumped out of the chair and flung herself into his arms.

Archimedes congratulated himself on the discipline not to toss her away from him. Instead, he awkwardly patted her back.

Not removing his gloves, of course.

"What's the matter, my dear?"

"My boss is still in the coma." Her voice choked. "They don't know if he'll ever wake up."

With a concerned expression—one Archimedes had fine-tuned from years of looking in a mirror—he forced his lips to touch her temple.

He'd have to disinfect himself when he returned home.

Rose nestled against him, rubbing at him. His body shuddered, not from desire, from disgust.

"Will he recover?"

Not that Archimedes cared. The point had been for a message to be delivered. And that had been accomplished.

She clung even tighter to him. "Now, dear, everyone is watching."

At the soft admonition, she flushed. Such a good girl. If he hadn't known Lyssa was his, he might have trained Rose properly, but she wasn't smart enough, not poised enough, not perfect enough. No match for him.

"I'm sorry." She stepped away from him and turned to the table. Quickly, she adjusted his silverware, placed the breadbasket in the precise center of the table, then wiped down his chair and waited for him to sit before seating herself.

Her fingers folded and refolded the napkin on the table.

He sent her a pointed glance. She sighed and placed her hands in her lap.

"You don't understand," she whispered. "They still can't find his most important *client*. The one I told you about. They're desperate."

"I haven't seen anything on the news," he commented, motioning for the waiter. When the man hurried over, he didn't glance at Rose. "We'll have the salmon. See that it's not overcooked. Two garden salads. No tomatoes. No cheese. No croutons. Dressing on the side. Three table-spoons exactly."

The waiter skittered away.

"The authorities have no idea where she is?" he asked, tugging his tracking monitor into view. Still at the UN. Inside he smiled. He relished the image of the WitSec authorities scrambling.

"No idea. They had me go through Marshal Nichols's computer and desk." She leaned forward. "I found a hidden drawer. It's locked. And there are files on his computer I can't decrypt. Tomorrow I have to call his boss. They're going to think I'm too stupid to know what Mr. Nichols was doing." A tear slid down her cheek. "What if they fire me?"

Her watery blue eyes gazed up at him. Archimedes smiled gently when all he wanted to do was stop her from speaking, giving away her weakness. "I helped you fix the computer a few weeks ago," he said softly.

The hope on her face widened his grin. "Would you like my assistance again?"

"You'd come with me?" She bit her lip. "We could get into trouble."

"We know how to get in without anyone knowing, don't we, Rose?"

She flushed. "You kissed me for the first time in my office after you sneaked in after hours."

"This time, we may do even more," he said, lowering his voice to a tempting whisper.

The waiter returned, placing the plate three inches from the edge of the table. Rose hurriedly adjusted the salad to precisely two inches.

"Well done, my dear." He glanced at his watch. "Let's finish our meal. By this time tomorrow, you will be able to share the information and be a hero."

"Thank you, sir," she said quietly.

"No, Rose. Thank you. You've given me more than you realize. I cannot wait to show my appreciation in a way you deserve."

JACK'S HOUSE HADN'T changed—except for the mess. Noah had only been here a few times. It was a family house, an old restored farmhouse. His friend could have made a good life here with Lyssa. He should have.

Noah took in her stiff posture as she stared into the cupboard above the refrigerator. "You sure there's nothing up there?"

She stepped off the stool, her expression wistful, but only for an instant. "Nothing but memories. Nothing I need."

She lied.

He said nothing, but the recognition she still held back tore at him. He wanted to either kiss her or shake her, to force her to reveal the truth, but now wasn't the time. Or the place.

"I want to scope out the house before we set the trap," he said. "Are you ready to go into the living room?"

She nodded and he pushed through the archway.

He remembered the scene all too well. The fine black

powder of fingerprint dust clung to the furniture, covered by a light layer of regular dust. A large area of the carpet had been cut out, but the rust of bloodstains still remained, surrounding the empty square.

He shot a glance at Lyssa. She didn't say anything but hugged her arms around her body and stared at the spot where Jack had died. She paused at the dinner table, still set in the corner, though a glass had broken and silverware had scattered, candles turned over.

Her tortured gaze met Noah's. "We were planning a special night," she said softly.

"I know," he said, his voice full of regret.

"We're going to get him, Jack," she whispered into the empty room. "I promise you."

"Just bedrooms upstairs?" Noah asked. "If I remember right."

With a curt nod, she padded toward the stairs.

"The master bedroom?" he asked.

"Down that hallway. This floor."

"A second entrance?"

"French doors in the master."

"We need to make sure we have an escape route we can use, but that he can't sneak in," Noah said. "Let's take a look there first."

Lyssa paused.

Noah clasped her by the shoulders. "Only a few more minutes, Lyssa. Keep your eye on the goal."

She led him to a closed door. Noah stepped in front of her. He used the scanner on the doorway. "Just checking," he said.

Carefully, he turned the knob and eased open the bedroom door.

He stilled.

Lyssa leaned around him. "Oh, my God!"

"Out," he shouted. "Now."

A pair of severed feet sat in the center of the bed with one message painted on the wall. In blood.

You're getting warmer.

ARCHIMEDES SPOONED A last bit of lemon gelato to cleanse his palate.

A small alarm sounded on his phone. He paused. That shouldn't have happened.

He pulled out his tracking device. Alessandra was still near the UN.

He typed in a code on his phone. An image flashed on the screen.

Alessandra. Sitting by yet another man.

In the house.

He panned the camera. Noah Bradford stood nearby.

"I-is something wrong, sir?" Rose asked quietly.

With everything inside him, Archimedes struggled not to toss the table. He picked up a wineglass. The crystal shattered in his hand, slicing his finger.

She leaped from her chair, but he waved her off.

"We're leaving," he said, standing, throwing down two hundred-dollar bills. He escorted Rose out of the restaurant.

Noah Bradford had done this. He had no doubt.

The man wanted to *try* to outsmart him. They were in for a very rude awakening.

IF ANYTHING ABOUT this situation were normal, the house would have been swarming with cops. As it was, after scanning the perimeter, Noah had called in Zane. Rafe had made it back from New York in record time.

They were all inside, the gruesome evidence still sitting in the bedroom.

"I wish Elijah were here," Zane said. "From what I can

tell, it looks like the feet were severed while the poor guy was still alive." He glanced at Noah. "Archimedes is a serious pycho."

"He's playing us," Noah said, his jaw tight.

"Finish the photographs," Noah ordered. "We'll send them to Elijah. I need to check something out, then we're out of here."

Noah sent Rafe a telling look. One thing about working with a man for a long time, they could almost read each other's minds. His friend distracted Lyssa and Noah eased past them, silently. He wanted a look in that cabinet.

He climbed the stool and opened the door.

A cookie jar. A couple of vases. One porcelain base was slightly off the circle of wood surrounded by dust. She'd moved it aside.

Noah shifted the piece, revealing two silhouettes surrounded by a thick layer of dust.

The print of a small shoe—a baby's shoe, and right next to it the outline of a rattle. He stilled, his mind whirling.

She didn't have a child. Not that he knew of.

He knew she and Jack had wanted kids. It was one reason his friend had put in for a transfer to a desk job.

But why remove them now?

Noah stepped to the ground. His phone rang and he glanced at the screen. His brother.

His gut sank. He had a bad feeling.

"What's up, Chase?"

"Noah, Sierra's missing."

Chapter Ten

"Rafe, get in here!"

Lyssa jerked at the panic in Noah's voice. She'd never heard that tone before.

Obviously Rafe and Zane never had either. They raced into the kitchen. One look at Noah's face, expression frozen, but eyes…oh, God, his eyes. The pain hurt her.

He flicked on the speakerphone. "Say that again, Chase. I've got Rafe with me."

"Our sister sneaked out and went to your place, Noah. W-we found her Jeep, but she's…she's just gone."

Noah paced back and forth, and Lyssa could nearly feel his panic.

"Get away from there, Chase. Now."

"I'm calling the police," Chase said.

A beep sounded through Noah's speaker. His hand tensed round the phone. "I'll call you right back. Just don't go into the house. Get the hell away from there." He flicked the flash button. "Bradford."

"This is Archimedes. You're playing a dangerous game, Mr. Bradford. You've changed the rules."

Noah's knuckles whitened. "Maybe." He motioned to Zane, but the computer tech was already at his laptop furiously typing away.

Lyssa clutched at the phone, but Noah placed his finger

on his lips. She wanted to scream and yell, but Noah held on to his emotions with a strength she couldn't fathom. His eyes had turned icy, though.

"You're probably a good liar most of the time, Mr. Bradford. You can't fool me." Archimedes paused, dragging out every second of torture. "I know you. Your family is your weakness."

Noah didn't say a word.

"You have discipline. Well, so do I, but I won't keep you in suspense. Tell me, Mr. Bradford, did you love your sister?"

Lyssa couldn't stop the gasp from escaping her mouth. Noah quickly pressed the mute button, but not quick enough.

"Alessandra, my love. At last we speak in person again." The man's voice purred through the phone. "I've sent you messages. All you have to do is decipher them and you'll find me."

"Don't say a word," Noah hissed.

Lyssa chewed on her lower lip and nodded.

Noah unmuted the phone. "Where's Sierra?" he said quietly.

Lyssa could tell he wanted to reach through the phone and strangle the man.

"Oh, she's not dead yet. You have a chance to save her."

"What do you want?" Noah bit the words out.

"Simple for a man of your intelligence. All you have to do, Mr. Bradford, is leave Connecticut. Go back to Denver. Once I know you're in Colorado and away from Alessandra, I'll contact you with your sister's location. But let me be clear. Your sister doesn't have a lot of time left. You should hurry."

Noah's expression grew fierce. He looked at Zane. The man shook his head. *Keep him talking,* he mouthed.

"I need a guarantee," Noah said. "How do I know—?"

"Don't insult my intelligence, Mr. Bradford. Your clumsy efforts to trace the signal won't get you anywhere. And Alessandra, I expect you to behave from now on. Haven't you learned yet that you *will* be mine?"

Lyssa couldn't speak. The man on the phone chuckled. "By the way, you might want to check the location where your friends left the tracking device. I've provided you another clue. We will meet soon, Alessandra. I'll be disappointed if you aren't smart enough to decipher it. Very disappointed."

The phone went silent. Noah stared down at Lyssa. She wanted to throw up. All of this was because of her. And she had no idea what to do about it. She backed away from him. "Go, Noah. Go home."

"I don't have a choice," Noah said aloud, then his narrowed gaze met Rafe's. The man smiled, but his eyes were deadly.

She didn't know what the look meant, but Rafe immediately walked out of the room. He returned with a suitcase in hand. Lyssa noticed Rafe's hand subtly signaling Noah.

"I'm sorry, Lyssa. Family comes first."

She understood, but a chill swept through her. He clasped her hand and met her gaze. He didn't say a word. She simply nodded.

"He's won then, hasn't he? I guess it's back to plan A. I find him."

She walked out the back door.

Noah, Rafe and Zane followed. Noah didn't speak until they reached the vehicle. Rafe scanned the interior. They piled in and Rafe turned to Noah. "He had the place bugged. I didn't take it out."

"Did you see a camera?"

Rafe shook his head. "Zane's better at spotting the electronics, but it wouldn't surprise me."

"Zane, get to the UN. Find out what Archimedes has left us. Rafe, in the meantime, you and I are switching places."

Lyssa stared at them. "What are you talking about?"

"Archimedes isn't dictating this investigation. Rafe's going to find Sierra—as me. I'm staying with you and we'll make this guy regret the day he ever came after you."

THE OUT-OF-THE-WAY motel wasn't Noah's normal style, but Rafe…well, Rafe stayed anyplace that no one would expect. His friend had lost so much, Noah got it. Rafe didn't have a home base or a permanent address—except for CTC.

For now, Noah would behave exactly like his friend. Except he had Lyssa with him.

She hovered by the door while he swept the room for surveillance.

"We're safe."

"For the moment," she said. "Noah—"

He looked over at her, knowing what she saw, the fake beard, the eye patch. He and Rafe had switched places. They'd done it before. With similar sizes and builds the misdirection had come in handy more than once. It hadn't taken long to get Rafe on the next flight to Denver, looking more like Noah than Noah himself. Clean-shaven, sunglasses to conceal the small patch he'd rigged over his eye.

"We're here for the night, Lyssa." Noah sat on the bed. "Why don't you take a shower. I need to call my family."

She hesitated for a moment, picked up her duffel and nodded. "I understand."

She disappeared into the bathroom. Noah rubbed the bridge of his nose. A text came through. From Zane. He'd been using highly illegal means to track unknown queries about Rafe's flight.

Sure enough, a sophisticated request had just come through. Zane hadn't been able to trace the originating computer—no surprise there—but they knew Archimedes was following them.

For now, they'd succeeded.

Zane had headed to the UN, Elijah was in D.C. following up on leads, and Noah and Alessandra were alone.

In a motel room.

Spraying water sounded from the bathroom. His gut twisting with trepidation, Noah picked up the new prepaid cell phone and dialed a number.

"Chase Bradford," his brother said, voice raspy with fatigue and worry.

"It's Noah."

"Where the hell have you been?" Chase shouted. "Sierra needs you. We need you. Are you on your way?"

Noah closed his eyes. "Archimedes took Sierra."

For a long moment, Chase said nothing. "The serial killer? Oh, God, no." Chase lowered his voice. "Is she…?"

"Listen carefully, Chase. This is about me. Archimedes wants me off the case I'm involved with. He's using Sierra as leverage."

"So, when you come home, he'll let her go?"

Noah gripped the phone hard. "I don't know."

His brother didn't say a word.

"Look, there's a chance," Noah said. "He told me she's alive. If we can find her first—"

"So, when will you get here?" Chase interrupted. "We'll pick you up. You obviously know this guy's methods."

Noah rubbed the back of his neck, the pain eating away at him. "I can't come home, Chase. Lyssa, the woman I'm protecting, needs me, too. The only way to stop this is to catch Archimedes, and he wants Lyssa."

"You're choosing some woman over our sister? Do I even know you? Are you part of this family or not?"

The words cut through his core.

"I'm sending Rafe Vargas. Look for me when the flight lands. He's in disguise, and Archimedes has to believe it." Noah rattled off the details. "Treat him like family. He knows as much as I do about Archimedes."

"Oh, so I just substitute some guy I don't know for my brother and that makes it okay? Are you out of your mind?"

"The killer promised that if I left Lyssa, he'd tell us where Sierra is. I'm giving him what he wants and hoping I can save Lyssa's life in the process. She's lost everything, Chase."

"You're playing with Sierra's life, Noah."

Noah rose from the bed and paced the floor. "It'll work. He's trying to set a trap for Lyssa. I need to be here for her, Chase. I have to.

He had to give them the truth. How was he supposed to choose between his sister and the woman he…damn, the woman he *loved*.

"Chase, this is what I do. It's the job I've never told you about. And Lyssa, she's…she's important to me. I can't explain more now, but I will. I promise."

"Noah, it's Mitch. I hear you. We'll find her, but Dad's going out of his mind. We can't put him off. What do we say?"

"The truth. I've learned the hard way that anything less gets you nowhere."

"Truth, then. What are Sierra's chances?"

The water from the shower stopped, but Noah didn't turn around. "I don't know. I think she's alive because he wanted me away from Lyssa. As long as we can keep the pretense going, we have a chance." Noah peered out the motel room window, then closed the curtains. "Sierra's smart. And resourceful. Check her phone, check anything she might have with her. She'll signal you if she can." Noah gripped the phone. "I want to be there," he said. "Believe that."

"Come home soon, Noah," Mitch said. "If the worst happens...we'll need you."

His brother hung up. With a low curse, Noah tossed the phone on the bedside table. The motel room was silent. The bathroom door snicked. Noah stiffened then looked over his shoulder.

Lyssa stood just inside the bedroom, hair wet, wearing a large T-shirt that left little to the imagination. Her eyes glistened with emotion. She took two steps toward him and launched herself into his arms. "I'm so sorry. There's nothing I can say but I'm incredibly sorry I ever involved you."

Like he'd had a choice. He wrapped his arms around her. God, he needed her. Noah buried his head into her shoulder. He'd tried to keep his emotions under control, but the thought of his baby sister at the hands of that madman... The big brother in him wanted to sob, the Falcon wanted to kill Archimedes with his bare hands, the man in him wanted to forget.

The man won.

He clutched her, lifted his head and fastened his lips to hers. She didn't whimper or pull away. She held him tight against her.

With a desperation that had been building over days, if not years, Noah's mouth explored hers, not tentatively, but taking her sweetness with a fierceness he didn't recognize. He'd imagined his first time loving her gentle and reverent, but he needed more from her.

He needed everything.

He raised his head, his heart racing, his breathing quick and shallow. "If you don't want this, tell me now, Lyssa. I won't be able to stop."

She placed her hands on the sides of his face, her lips already swollen from his kiss. She pressed her mouth to his then didn't say a word. She simply pulled the T-shirt over her head and dropped it to the floor.

His body leaped in response. Her skin still damp and warm, the smooth silkiness beckoned him. He couldn't wait. Noah lifted her into his arms and strode over to the bed, throwing down the spread and laying her gently on the sheets. Quickly, he stripped off his clothes and settled his hard, urgent body on top of her.

With emotions quivering at the surface, Noah lowered his head to her breast and tasted her curves, his hands exploring every inch of skin.

Lyssa arched against him, her hands tugging his head closer, massaging his scalp and moving down to his shoulders. With a low groan, he teased her nipple, the taut bud responding beautifully to his caress. With a small nip, a low moan escaped from her.

"More," she breathed against him.

He eased down her body, his desire flaring out of control. He scraped his teeth across her belly and eased her legs apart. She didn't resist. With a low growl he tasted her, relishing her response to him.

The reality of Lyssa in his arms was better than any fantasy or dream.

"Please," her voice shook. She tugged him back up then hooked her heels around his hips, arching against him, begging for his possession.

Slowly, tenderly, he entered her, using every ounce of willpower not to slam into her and lose himself. He stilled, watching her hooded lids blink, her lips part, her back arch.

"More," she ordered.

That one word eradicated his control. Passion took over, taking them on a ride where the world vanished. She wrapped her arms and legs around him and buried her face into his shoulder, meeting him thrust for thrust, touch for touch.

The friction erupted into flames, engulfing them, taking them higher and higher until the world exploded between them.

Noah collapsed on top of Lyssa, his body spent, his breathing unsteady. Her heart raced and she stroked his hair as they came down to earth.

He could barely move, she felt so good beneath him, but he would crush her. He shifted his weight off her and she groaned.

"Did I hurt you?" he asked, pushing strands of damp hair away from her face.

She shook her head and moved, rolling him onto his back, setting her body over his.

Oh, yeah, this was much better.

He searched her face for a hint of regret. He might have been dreaming of this for years, but it had happened fast. He couldn't be sorry, but...

"Oh no you don't," Lyssa said, leaning over him, pressing her naked breasts against his chest, grinding her hips against his. "I can see those analytical gears grinding. Don't think for a minute I didn't want this as much as you did."

"You're too perceptive for your own good," Noah muttered, but still he looked away.

She caught his chin in her fingertips and forced him to meet her gaze. "What are you thinking?"

Should he tell her the truth, what he truly feared? He

caressed the silkiness of her hair and hugged her closer, partly so he didn't have to look into her eyes.

He rested his chin on the top of her hair, letting himself believe for a few moments that she belonged in his arms for always.

"Can I tell you later?" he asked quietly.

"I won't wait forever," she said softly, pushing up so she could see his face. "Let me start. I didn't do this because I feel guilty, even though I do. I didn't make love with you to take your mind off your troubles. And last—" she leaned closer, nipping at his ear "—I know you're not Jack."

Noah stiffened beneath her. She'd touched on the real problem. It had been a long time since she'd thought of Noah as anything like Jack. She'd loved Jack, loved him deeply. She'd never forget him, but her heart stuttered when Noah spoke. It had almost killed her when she realized Archimedes had hurt his family. She would have felt guilt, no matter what, but it was as if Noah's pain had crept into her soul.

She still couldn't believe he hadn't just pushed her aside.

He brought his hands to her arms and she knew he was about to move her away. She gripped his waist between her legs, bracing her hands against his chest.

"Are you trying to trap me?" he asked, raising a brow.

"I'm not letting you get away until you believe me."

"We've been together nonstop for days. The situation is intense," Noah added. "It's natural we would turn to each other, lean on each other."

"Don't even say it," Lyssa whispered.

"Why now?" Noah asked.

"Because for the first time since this started, *you* needed *me*," she said simply.

Noah's phone buzzed on the bedside table. Lyssa

groaned and reached across him to pick it up. She handed him the phone.

"Bradford."

"You know those feet we found?" Zane said, his voice loud enough for her to hear. "I have the body. And there's something you need to see."

THE UNITED NATIONS building loomed closer, flashing lights of emergency vehicles blocking the street. The cab slowed to a stop. Lyssa stepped out of the vehicle. He hadn't wanted to risk Archimedes identifying their car. They'd left it in a parking garage on the edge of the city.

Noah paid the driver and stepped onto the street, shrugging into Rafe's persona even deeper. Yes, he wore the eye patch and beard, but even the way he stood and walked reminded her of the former Green Beret. Dangerous.

"Slow and easy," he said to her, keeping his distance. He was Rafe Vargas not Noah Bradford. He would treat her as such.

She tried not to take it personally. She wanted to hold on to him, feel his strength and his warm touch.

Instead, she shoved her hands into her pockets. With the security at the UN, she couldn't carry her gun. She hated feeling so vulnerable.

They walked past the police cars and toward the front entrance. She sent him a sidelong glance.

She didn't know how he felt. He'd shut down after the phone call. Once again, pushing her away. His eerie ability to transform himself into another man gave him the tools to become the Falcon. It was the mask he wore. She didn't know if she'd ever penetrate the crack in his emotions again. For a brief moment she'd seen beyond the Falcon, beyond the computer genius. Beyond the man who was determined to save her life.

An hour ago he'd held her as if he never wanted to let her go. She couldn't remember feeling more needed or desired.

Now he was an acquaintance. He was a man who she'd hired to help her. She'd believed she found the real Noah, but could she ever be sure?

Tension pulsed from his body as he escorted her to the entrance. Yellow crime-scene tape draped near a door just inside.

Two guards stepped in their path. "Move along."

"We have business—" Noah began.

"They're with me." Zane motioned them in.

The guards stepped aside.

"Ransom pulled some strings," Zane said quietly. "Otherwise, I'd be sitting in jail right now lawyering up."

"Good thing we have friends with even more powerful friends," Noah said.

His words barely registered. Lyssa hadn't been in the lobby of the building for two years. Very little had changed. "He wants to destroy everything about my past, doesn't he?"

She'd imagined herself doing important work in this building. No matter what happened, she'd never come back here.

Zane led them over to a closet. "Can you give us a minute?" he asked a pair of investigators. "She might be able to identify him."

They stepped aside.

"Brace yourself. It's not pretty," Zane warned.

Lyssa stepped closer and peered into the small room.

The gruesome remainder of a man's body sat propped up inside, positioned as if staring straight ahead. Her eyes dropped to the symbols carved into his chest.

"Infinity," she whispered.

"Plus another symbol," Zane said.

A shape similar to a cursive *p* had been carved just below the man's naval. Lyssa's mind wouldn't stop whirling. She knew the symbol. What was Archimedes trying to tell her?

"I recognize it. Why can't I think?"

She knelt down, forcing herself to study the carving. It wasn't a perfect *p*. No, there were too many curves. It wasn't a rho either. More like a wonky *p* with a tail. More like...

Her thoughts went back to her last job at the UN.

"It's Sanskrit," she said, her voice harsh.

Zane stared down. "I'll be damned."

"The number nine."

"Numbers," Noah said. "Could the other symbols have meanings in other languages?"

"I think so. The epsilon could be Arabic for the number four."

She clutched Noah's arm. He glanced at her then she dropped her hand. She couldn't pretend they knew one another. Archimedes was probably watching.

"We're getting closer," Noah said. "Do you recognize him?"

"He looks familiar." She tried to avoid looking at his legs, but the gruesome sight of his missing feet drew her gaze. "Why?"

"He wants to make sure you're too afraid to deny him," Noah's hand drifted down her back, the small movement comforting, and invisible to anyone watching. "Can you remember where you met him?"

She studied his features. His face, the indentation in his chin, his hair.

His hair. The man's reddish-blond beard stabbed at Lyssa's memory. "Did he have any identification?"

Zane shook his head. "Nothing. They're running his prints. We should know something soon if he's ever worked in government, was in the military or had a record."

She studied the man's face more closely. His eyes were open, staring into space; his mouth was twisted in pain. "I know him. I'm certain of it."

Her gaze fell to the carnation on the collar of his shirt. "What about the flower?"

"Weird, huh," Zane said. "It was there when I got here."

"It's a carnation. A boutonniere. Oh, God." Lyssa couldn't believe it. "I know who he is."

Noah shot her a sharp glance.

"It's Bill Zeigler. He was my date. To my senior prom."

THE JUSTICE DEPARTMENT didn't go for cheap office furniture. Archimedes leaned back in U.S. Marshal Reid Nichols's executive leather chair.

The solid wood desk hadn't been a challenge, and right now Archimedes couldn't stop smiling. He replayed the airport-surveillance tape.

Noah Bradford had a distinctive walk, a slight hitch from an apparent injury to his left leg. Archimedes's nemesis had left New York and returned to Denver. He'd seen the man board the plane, and a quick hack into the reservations system had verified the ticket.

Alessandra belonged to Archimedes now. She would *finally* be his. Once Alessandra came to him, she would *never* run from him again.

As of thirty minutes ago, he knew exactly how to control her.

Reid Nichols's computer monitor blinked at him. He grinned again. He had everything he needed.

"Did you find something?" Rose's eyes were wide with hope. "Could you get at the files?"

"Oh, yes, my dear. I have exactly what I need now. Thank you."

Her brow wrinkled. "I don't understand."

"I know you don't." He sighed, memorized an address then turned off the computer. "You really shouldn't be so trusting, Rose. It's a flaw."

"But I love you. We're going to be together. Of course I trust you."

"Rose, Rose, Rose." Archimedes pulled a garrote from his pocket, his weapon of choice for those who talked too much—or not enough.

She stared down at the metal in his hand, utterly confused. The poor dear.

Then, as if she suddenly realized she should be very afraid, she stepped back.

Archimedes smiled. "Didn't you wonder why, after no one caring about you for the first thirty-five years of your life, I happened to sweep you into my arms? Didn't it give you pause that a few weeks after we began dating and I came to your office, Alessandra Cummings was found?"

Slowly, Rose shook her head. "No. You love me. I know you do."

"I don't love anyone except Alessandra." He could see the truth seeping into her limited brain. He stepped closer. "I do, however, enjoy a woman's fear and watching the life drain from her eyes as I kill her."

Rose whirled around and grabbed the doorknob. He smiled at her struggle with the brass handle. Before she could undo the lock, he gripped her by the hair and shoved her up against the wall.

"Please, don't do this," she whispered. "Please, Todd."

"Never say my name," he rasped into her ear.

"Todd, you don't want to hurt me," she whispered.

"Yes, Rose, I do."

She tried to shove her knee against his groin, but she obviously had no idea how. He plunged a hypodermic into her skin. Within seconds she sagged against him, sliding down the wall. "Please. What did I do?"

"You know me," he said softly, looping the metal wire around her throat. "Surely by now, you know who I am."

He tightened the noose. Her eyes widened. She gasped. Her hands clutched at his coat.

"Todd." She choked, sucking in breaths. "Please."

"Beg me, Rose. Beg for your life."

Her grip loosened. "P-please."

"Say my name. The name the entire world fears."

"A…Archimedes." A tear rolled down her cheek.

"Yes." He tightened the wire. "Can you feel the ecstasy, Rose? Give me what I want, because you will die."

Terrified, her gaze darted around the room. A shiver of pleasure ran through him. "Yes, my dear. You're dying now."

Thirty seconds more and the life faded from her eyes.

He shuddered in satisfaction as the last glimmer vanished.

"Thank you, Rose."

He pocketed the garrote, let her drop to the ground and without a backward glance walked out the door.

Chapter Eleven

Noah couldn't get Lyssa out of the UN building fast enough. He bundled her into a cab before ordering the driver to take the long way back to the motel. Zane would have to charm the Crime Scene Unit then find his own way. They had some symbols to decipher.

By the time they made it to the motel it was two in the morning. Noah paid off the taxi, watching the vehicle disappear into the night so he could be certain no one could connect them to the room number. After a quick scan of the door and room, Noah entered, finally motioning Lyssa inside. She couldn't stop the shivering. He turned up the heat and pulled her against him, rubbing her arms and back to warm her up.

He'd intended to get right to work, but she huddled against him, seeking warmth and something more.

"How soon will Zane be here?" she asked, looking first at him then the unmade bed, her green eyes dark with longing.

No way could Noah resist the invitation. He lowered his mouth to hers, wanting just a sweet taste. But her lips parted eagerly beneath his and a low rumble sounded from within his chest.

Her arms wound around his neck, pulling him closer. Noah didn't hesitate. He explored her mouth, needed to feel her. She was his dream. He backed her to the bed and she sank into the mattress. He followed her down, and she cradled his weight as if they were meant to be together.

They fit.

Lyssa arched against him, pulling him closer. He could lose himself so easily. He wanted the world to disappear, just for a while.

As if the universe laughed at his hopes, Noah's phone intruded once again. His body straining against hers, he kissed her one last time then sighed, taking a few calming deep breaths before pulling away. "Zane will be here soon. That was his text."

He shifted his hips off hers, propped himself on his arm and kissed her nose. "You're dangerous to my equilibrium."

She stroked his arm, looking up at him. "I needed to know if what happened between us was real."

"Oh, yeah, it's definitely real," he said. "Too real."

He groaned and rolled out of bed. "But unless you want Zane to know exactly how we spent our evening, we should probably make the bed."

She stepped over the spread, her cheeks flaming. Within a few minutes they'd tucked the spread around the pillows and smoothed the wrinkles.

"I better set up the computer," he said, powering it on and setting up the secure internet. "You're brilliant, you know. How many people would recognize written Sanskrit?"

"If I were smarter, I'd have figured this out before poor Bill was killed."

"Come here," he said, his voice husky, pulling her closer for another kiss. "Without you, we wouldn't have a lead at all. Take the compliment."

A sharp knock sounded at the door. Noah left her standing by the computer, pulled out his Glock and answered the door.

Zane walked in. He looked down at her then straight at Noah, his brow arched. With a hooded glance, Noah took in Lyssa's appearance. She looked thoroughly kissed; there was no denying it. So much for keeping the relationship hidden.

He cleared his throat. "Have a seat."

Zane popped the top on a can of soda and tugged his laptop from his bag without saying anything except with his eyes. *Bad idea. She's in danger; it could cause trouble.* Noah's head might agree. His heart didn't give a damn.

He pulled out a sheet of paper and scratched a spiral on it. "Let's assume each symbol stands for a single number or letter. We think the fourth is a nine."

"Is the third just an *E?*" Zane asked.

"I think Lyssa was right before. Let's try four. Arabic."

"You really believe he went to the trouble of using different languages?" Zane asked.

"Lyssa speaks several languages, she was a UN translator. In a twisted way it makes sense," Noah said.

"In a psycho's head, I guess."

"Your point?" Noah asked.

"The first symbol was on Chastity's notepad. A spiral."

Zane tapped a few keys into Noah's computer. She leaned forward and pointed to the screen. "There it is—the spiral looks just like the number three in Bengali."

"Damn," Zane commented.

"The second doesn't look like modern writing. More like hieroglyphics or pictographs."

"But it resembles something I've seen in Belize," Noah said. "Try Mayan."

Zane typed in a few keystrokes. "There we have it. A bar and three dots. Eight."

"Three—eight—four—nine." Lyssa mused. "What does it mean?"

"The beginning of a phone number, an address? It could be almost anything," Zane said, drumming his fingers on the laptop. "Even a code."

Lyssa stared at the sequence. "I don't recognize it." She let out a sigh. "Are we even on the right track? What if they *are* letters?"

Zane's secure phone rang. He pressed the speakerphone. "Westin."

"Is Noah with you?" Rafe asked. "I didn't want to use his number since Archimedes used it."

"You're on speaker." Noah didn't like the sound of his friend's voice. He braced himself. "Sierra?"

A frustrated sigh reached through from Denver. "Archimedes called. I have a web address. You need to see this."

Noah's entire body stilled. "Send it."

Within seconds, Zane clicked on the link.

A grainy image appeared.

Noah went deathly still.

Sierra lay in the floor of a small room, her hands and feet bound, her mouth duct taped. Her shirt was open and an infinity symbol had been carved near her breastbone. Her eyes were closed.

"Is she—" Noah couldn't finish the sentence.

"She's breathing. We can tell that much. She hasn't opened her eyes, though."

"That son of a bitch," Noah bit out. "Where is she?"

"We don't know." Noah had never heard Rafe so edgy. "But I'm going to find her. I need to trace the signal. Your father tried but he ended up bouncing around Pakistan. I need Zane's help."

"You got it," Noah said. He clutched the phone in his hand. He turned to Zane. "Find my sister. Take away his leverage."

NOAH PAID FOR a second motel room so Zane could process the video and audio through his high-tech equipment. Noah left his friend alone, muttering at the computer, earphones on and staring at the screen.

He fought not to slam the door open to Lyssa's motel room in frustration. Shoulders heavy with doubt, he sat on the bed. He should be in Denver, with his family. But if he left, Lyssa was dead.

As if reading his mind, she sat beside him, reaching for his hand. "Rafe will find her. We have to believe that."

The quiet words held hope, but Noah couldn't feel it. "Yeah. If Archimedes doesn't decide she's better off dead than alive."

Lyssa winced, pulling away. "I wish—"

"Don't say anything." He reached for her hands. "I'm sorry. It's not your fault. It's mine."

"Aren't you the one who told me Archimedes holds the blame?"

Noah stood, pacing the small room, unable to light anywhere. "Don't confuse me with my own logic," he said, his voice laced with bitter humor he didn't try to hide. "I had a disagreement with the family a few days ago. They couldn't contact me...they were worried. They didn't know anything about my—" he paused "—extracurricular activities for CTC. If I'd told them the whole truth, maybe Sierra would have taken more precautions. He might not have been able to take her."

"You did what you thought was best," Lyssa said, walking into his arms.

She rested her head on his shoulder quietly for a few moments.

"Is that why you're keeping your secret?" he asked softly. "For the best?"

She stilled and clutched his shirt. "Yes."

He stroked her hair, its softness caressing his hand. "Don't make my mistake."

Lyssa backed away. "It's not the same. You don't understand."

"Then explain it to me. How do you know I can't help?"

"Helping would make things worse. Helping might lead him to—" She took in a shaky breath. "I can't say the words, Noah. I promised myself. I promised Jack."

His best friend's name robbed him of his breath worse than a blow to the gut. What was he supposed to say to that?

A rap sounded on the door, then another patterned knock.

Lyssa met Noah's gaze, unwavering, certain. His suspicions percolated. God, he prayed he was wrong.

Noah stalked across the room and answered the door. "Did you locate Sierra?"

The computer expert shook his head. "We were updating Elijah. He had news of his own. A woman's body was found inside the lobby of the Justice Department."

Lyssa gasped.

"The mole?"

"That's Elijah's guess. She'd worked for Reid since he moved to D.C. Her name was Rose Wright."

"Can we connect—"

"That's not all, Noah. Rose was murdered exactly like Frederick Allen. Garrote. And there was a note attached to her body. A message for Lyssa. From Archimedes."

She slipped her hand into Noah's, squeezing tight. "What does he want?"

"He left an address and a box number. Archimedes wants you in Alexandria, Virginia. Today."

LYSSA DIDN'T WANT to be here. Not on this plane; not going anywhere near Alexandria. Her nerves were shattered. She could barely breathe. Too close, they were going too close. She'd never been more terrified in her life.

Her leg bounced up and down as she stared out the window, the sun having risen during the flight. This couldn't be happening.

"Lyssa," Noah said. "Buckle up."

Absently, she fastened her seat belt.

He knelt in front of her. "Look at me."

Reluctantly, she met his gaze. "What's going on?"

She just shook her head. "I…I can't. Please don't ask me again."

His jaw tightened, he rose and buckled in.

She closed her eyes against the horror that suffocated her. Archimedes had taken Noah's sister. The woman might already be dead. So how would revealing the truth help?

She glanced at the air phone sitting next to her in the Lear. Was she wrong? Should she call Mary? Wouldn't that be playing into Archimedes's hands? She hadn't contacted her best friend from high school since graduation prior to a call begging for help two years ago. Nothing should tie them together.

With desperation she'd asked Reid to run a background check on Mary. Lyssa had taken a huge chance, but she'd had no choice.

And now they were flying within a couple of hours of the high school where Lyssa had met Mary, where she'd met her prom date, Bill. Where they'd all gone to high school, and where Lyssa's daughter now lived with a new identity—and her other mother.

She sent a sidelong glance at Noah. The disappointment on his face hurt her heart. She rubbed her eyes. How could she choose? If anything happened to Jocelyn, she'd never forgive herself.

The Lear's wheels touched down. The moment they exited the plane, an SUV pulled up. Elijah.

"Thought you needed backup," he said with a frown. He grimaced. "Sorry about your sister, Noah."

"Update," Noah responded, his voice curt.

"Sierra seems to be safe enough. For the moment."

"I'm texting with my family. I know how she is. What about Rose Wright?"

"No leads, but the murder happened at a different location. Justice is locked down tight. No one's talking."

"So, basically, no leads."

Elijah's jaw clenched. "Except the address Archimedes provided in his note. It's on the south side in a sketchy section of Columbia Heights. The feds wanted to stake it out."

Noah blasted a curse through the vehicle. "They could cost Sierra her life."

"Ransom made a call. He's got some friends in very high places."

Noah nodded. "How long do we have?"

"Hard to tell. There's a lot of pressure."

"How about Reid?" Lyssa asked. "Any news?"

"They've taken him off the drugs. Hopefully he wakes up soon. It's hard to tell."

Noah grunted, and for the first time he met Lyssa's gaze. She recognized the emotions flaring in his eyes. Frustration, anger, accusation. And betrayal. She'd have to accept she'd ruined any chance of a future with him.

She did trust Noah. She'd made herself more vulnerable to him than anyone since Jack. She just didn't trust Archimedes.

Elijah turned the car onto a street. A mailbox and copy shop sat at the corner. They passed the store then turned onto a new street. "I scoped it out before I picked you up. The place has surveillance. We should assume he's watching."

"He'll see Rafe walk in and retrieve whatever he has for us in the box." Noah reached out to open the car door.

Lyssa clutched his arm. "I should do it."

He glared at her. "You're not going in there."

"What if it's a trap? A bomb?"

"I'll be fine." Noah pinned Elijah with his gaze. "Watch her. If it goes bad, I want you out of here. Get her to CTC."

Elijah tugged out his 1911 and nodded.

Noah exited the vehicle. Elijah turned to her. "What the hell is going on between you two?"

Lyssa gripped the armrest as he disappeared inside. "Nothing."

"I know you've had it rough, but Noah needs a clear head. His sister's in danger, you're in trouble. Don't make it worse. One too many distractions and this thing ends bad. You get me?"

Lyssa nodded.

Noah didn't take long. He carried an envelope and a prepaid cell phone. "It's clean. Take us to a motel room. We need internet access. And we have less than one hour until he contacts us."

ELIJAH CLOSED THEM into the motel room. Another Rafe special. Noah pulled out his laptop and set up the security. He glanced at his watch. "Thirty minutes."

Lyssa approached him. He stiffened in response. "What do you want?"

"Can we talk for a minute?" she asked hesitantly.

He couldn't imagine what they had to discuss. She'd made herself perfectly clear. When it came down to it, she couldn't believe in him. So be it. He'd do this job and that would be the end of it.

"There's nothing to discuss. Besides, Archimedes provided a web address, I need to set it up."

He turned his back on her, and his phone buzzed. He glanced at the receiver and put the phone to his ear. "Did you find her, Rafe?"

"Zane narrowed the signal to an old warehouse south of downtown. Lots of old buildings. Noah, she's awake."

Noah turned on the computer, opened the browser and went to the URL. Sierra's eyes were open. He could see the anger in her eyes—and the fear.

She looked up at the camera, turned over and arranged her hand as if she were holding a bottle.

"What's she doing?" Noah asked.

Sierra's hand moved again. She created a fist. Then she repeated the last movement.

"What is she trying to signal?" Noah asked.

A whisper sounded through the phone.

"Your brother thinks it's sign language. CTC."

"Get Ransom on the phone," Noah barked. "See what he knows about this."

"Does she know who you work for?" Rafe asked.

"I didn't think so."

Rafe cleared his throat. "Look, Noah, you need to be aware, the signal is coming from an area where there's a whole block of buildings scheduled for demolition. Today at noon."

Noah couldn't move. "Can you stop it?"

"Your father's calling in all kinds of favors. We're working it."

Elijah tapped his watch.

"Rafe—"

"I'll get her out. I promise." He hung up the phone.

"What's up?" Elijah asked.

"They're closing in on Sierra," he said.

"Thank God," Lyssa said.

"They don't have her yet."

Noah sat down and typed in the URL Archimedes had provided. The screen was blank. "I'm cutting the connection," he said. "We don't go in until the time. I don't want Archimedes to have a chance to trace us here."

Lyssa paced back and forth. She'd broken his heart. If the past few days had taught him anything it was that secrets weren't worth it. His mistakes may have cost Sierra her life. And he refused to give his heart to a woman who couldn't trust him.

She'd given him her body; she'd trusted him with her life, but she wouldn't trust him with her soul. He'd witnessed his father and mother together. They'd been a team, each other's best friends. The trust between them was never spoken. It was just there.

He wanted Lyssa, he couldn't deny that, but he wanted to spend his life with a woman who had complete faith in him.

Lyssa didn't.

A piece of his soul disintegrated with the realization. Somewhere inside of him he'd prayed someone like Lyssa would come along, someone he could share everything with, and here she was, a fantasy woman who drove his body wild, was everything he wanted—except the most important thing.

The wall he'd erected around his heart solidified. He'd finish this job and go back to CTC. That's where he belonged. The life his father had, the life his brother Mitch had found, it wasn't for him. He was expecting too much.

Lyssa approached him while Elijah worked on the computer, trying to pretend he wasn't listening.

"Are you going to talk to me again?" she asked.

"Of course."

She sighed. "I know you're upset—"

"Now's not the time. It's almost over, Lyssa. Then you can have your life back. And I'll have mine."

He stepped away from her tempting scent and pulled a signal booster and decryptor from his bag. Neither were on the market, they were in a testing phase. He'd come up with the idea when Daniel and his new wife had been lost in the desert of West Texas during a lightning storm. How to boost a signal and follow it.

Lyssa disappeared into the bathroom. He let out a long sigh.

"You two okay?" Elijah said quietly once she'd closed the door.

"Fine." Noah met his colleague's gaze. "I need this to be over."

"I don't know what's going on, but don't screw this up, Noah. She's something special."

"She doesn't trust me...us," he said, attaching the last connector into place. "I can't live that way."

"Lyssa's been on the run for two years."

Noah leaned forward. "How much do I have to prove that I can be trusted? She's keeping a secret from me, Elijah. A big one. I'm willing to die for her, and she can't tell me what she's hiding. That chips away at a guy's heart, you know."

"Yeah," Elijah said quietly. "I know. Been there. Without trust, there's nothing."

They both returned to work, letting the sour memories settle between them.

Ten minutes later, Lyssa appeared from the bathroom. Noah tried not to notice the red puffiness of her eyes.

"Are you ready?" he said.

She nodded.

At exactly nine o'clock, Noah opened the browser window and entered in the URL again. The black screen appeared.

One minute passed, then two minutes.

Lyssa paced back and forth and retrieved her shotgun. Elijah went to the window, perusing the parking lot.

"Is he out there?" she asked. "Is this just a trick to find us?"

The phone left in the mailbox rang.

"Answer it," Noah said.

She pressed the speakerphone. "H-hello?"

"Alessandra, my dear. You've been keeping secrets. You've been a very naughty girl."

LYSSA'S BREATH STOPPED. No. Reid was still unconscious. He was the only one who knew. She hadn't told Noah. She hadn't told anyone. He was bluffing. He had to be.

She met Noah's unyielding gaze.

"I...I don't understand."

"Don't lie to me, Alessandra. Don't *ever* lie to me. Your friend Mary lies. She disrespected me. She has to pay."

The screen blinked on.

Mary Patterson was strapped to a chair, her eyes dark with pain. Archimedes stood nearby, a strange smile protruding from the mouth of his balaclava.

Perfectly straight teeth. The odd thought flitted through Lyssa's mind even as disbelief washed through her.

No!

"Alessandra!" Mary cried into the camera. "God, I'm sorry."

Archimedes grabbed her chin. "Do you recognize your good friend, Alessandra? The person you trusted the most? She tried to lie, but she knows better now."

The camera panned down to Mary's hands. Two of her fingers were missing.

Lyssa's knees buckled.

"Don't you know I'm the only one who lives up to my promises, Alessandra?"

The camera panned to the left. A toddler sat crying in a Pack 'n Play, reaching to Mary.

"Marmie! Marmie!"

"God, no!" Lyssa moaned.

"That's right, Alessandra. I have your daughter."

Noah caught Lyssa when she fell. He cradled her in his arms. She gripped his arms, gaze frozen at the computer screen.

Archimedes repositioned the camera and leaned in. "Alessandra. Don't you want to know how to get your daughter back?"

She gripped the phone tight. "Please, don't hurt them." Tears streamed down Lyssa's face. She trembled in Noah's arms. "I'll do anything."

"That's better," he said, those teeth grinning in a way that made her shiver in revulsion. "First, you must understand that lies are unacceptable. For example…" Archimedes's voice trailed off.

"Your friend lied about the identity of your daughter to the world for eighteen months. She lied to me today. She still hasn't admitted the truth."

He clucked his tongue at Mary.

Lyssa froze at the resigned expression that settled on Mary's face. She covered the phone. "What's he doing?"

She couldn't see what Archimedes held in his hand.

"Please," Mary whispered. "Alessandra...tell my family—"

Mary's body seized in the chair. A flash sparked.

"Stop!" Lyssa shouted. "Stop it. What are you doing?"

"He's electrocuting her," Elijah shouted.

Seconds later, Mary's body sagged in the chair, her body charred.

Lyssa couldn't stop the sobs.

Archimedes chuckled. He panned the camera to Jocelyn. Her daughter was screaming, terrified.

"Please," she whispered into the phone.

The camera moved up. A symbol hung on the wall. Noah quickly copied the strangely shaped *v*.

"The time for running is over, Alessandra. Decipher my message if you want to live. Be at the rendezvous point in two hours with the answer and come alone." He smiled. "I hope you can decipher the clues, Alessandra.

"If you don't, your daughter will die."

Chapter Twelve

Noah propped Lyssa up and held her in his arms. Her desperation palpable, she clutched at him. "What does it mean?"

"The last symbol is Urdu," Noah said. "The number seven."

"Three—eight—four—nine—seven? We only have two hours."

He turned her to face him. "Look at me," he said softly. "Two hours isn't that long, so we know he's nearby. We'll figure it out.

"Hand me the laptop," Noah ordered Elijah. He entered the number into a search engine and scanned the list. "What has a five-digit number?"

Lyssa took a slow deep breath. "Addresses, phone numbers, zip code. She scribbled the number, placing dashes between the numbers, then slashes. "A date?" She scribbled. "The three could be March." She shook her head. "No, that doesn't work. 3/84/97."

"Wait a minute." Noah pulled up a spreadsheet. He entered the number then changed the format. "May 5, 2004?"

"Where'd you come up with that?" Elijah asked.

"It's how the spreadsheet tracks dates. The number of days from January 1, 1900." Noah turned to Lyssa. "Does it mean anything to you?"

"I graduated high school that year," she said. "At Thomas Jefferson High School here in Alexandria." She shook her head. "We graduated in June."

"What happened in May?" Noah asked.

She stood up, pacing back and forth. "Prom." Her eyes widened. "Bill."

"Where was the prom, Lyssa?"

"In the gym."

"Your rendezvous. You're going back to prom." Noah grabbed his bag and glanced at his watch. "We're running out of time."

LYSSA BUCKLED HER knife around her ankle and pulled out her shotgun. She looked over at Noah. "Are we right?"

"Bill was one of the victims. Archimedes cut his feet off. Yeah, this is about prom."

"How did you ever figure the date out?" she asked, still in awe.

"I told you I was a geek. I like spreadsheets."

She twisted around. Elijah's truck followed close. Zane was still in New York. CTC was sending a second team, but they wouldn't get here in time. "Hurry," she said. "Please."

"Why didn't you tell me about your daughter?" he asked finally.

He picked up speed heading toward Braddock. She let out a long, slow breath. "I've kept her a secret for so long. What if…what if he captured you, tortured you? I couldn't take the chance." She bowed her head. "I was just protecting her. I'm sorry, Noah. I couldn't risk it, even for you."

"We both tried our best to protect our family."

"And failed," she said. "I should have trusted you. I do trust you." She gripped his leg. "This guy has known me for ten years. I'm the reason Jack is dead. I'm the reason my daughter will never know her father. Help me end this." A shuddering breath escaped her. "For Jack. For our little girl."

Noah didn't say anything. Seconds ticked by.

"Noah?"

"For Jack," he said quietly. "And for you." He gunned the SUV and it sped up. "Did Jack know you were pregnant?"

"Her name is Jocelyn," Lyssa said. She couldn't stop the tears. "I was going to tell him that night. I had it all planned. A celebration dinner, and then I'd bring out my surprise."

"The rattle and baby shoes," Noah finished.

She gaped at him.

"I saw the outline in the dust at your place."

"You knew?"

"I suspected," he countered. "I didn't know if it was wishful thinking on your part or something more. Reid never said anything."

"His sister is a midwife. She delivered the baby then took her to Mary. That's the last time I held her. All she has of me are a few videos singing lullabies. I hoped, maybe someday, when we met again, she'd recognize my voice, or a song."

She clutched Noah's arm. "You have to promise me. Whatever happens to me, you get Jocelyn out of there. You make sure she's safe."

"Lyssa—"

"This isn't up for negotiation. If you have to make a choice, Noah, you choose Jocelyn. Not me."

"It won't come to that." Noah pulled to the side of the road. "We're two miles away. You have to drive from here alone. We need him to believe you're following orders. I'll be nearby, Lyssa."

She studied his face. She believed him. "I know."

"Your instincts will be to fight. Don't. He has a huge ego, but it's fragile. You need to be smart. Play up to him. Get him to lower his guard. I'll look for an opening."

"What if—"

"If I can't get at you for some reason, when he's vulnerable and least expects it, use the head butt, then I'll make his move."

"Run at him? I thought you said not to fight."

"The key is to surprise him. If you're docile, he won't expect it. Do you understand?"

She nodded.

"No halfways, Lyssa. Don't hesitate. Give it all your strength. If you use your body weight, it will knock him off center and give you enough time to get out of reach. I'll be there to take him out. I promise."

She reached for her knife. "I know what to do."

"We do this together."

Noah hugged her close, and she leaned into him, drawing from his strength. They'd get her daughter back. She had to trust in him.

"Be careful," he said.

She nodded.

He exited the SUV and Lyssa slid into the driver's seat. She rolled down the window. "I want your solemn promise, Noah. Jocelyn first."

"Jocelyn first," he said, his brow furrowed.

Noah walked behind her and disappeared into Elijah's truck.

Lyssa took a last glance in her rearview mirror and pulled forward. She hadn't been down these roads since her father had been reassigned right before graduation. Her parents had been killed six months later in a terrorist attack at the Spanish embassy.

She'd thought at the time nothing would ever be worse. How wrong she'd been.

"Prom? Who are you, Archimedes?"

Prom night was the last big event she'd attended in high school. She'd been so excited. Bill Zeigler had been the quarterback of the football team. She'd had a huge crush on him, and she couldn't believe when he'd actually asked her out.

Somehow, Archimedes knew about that night. She had no idea how or why.

Lyssa drove onto the large campus and headed toward the gym. She turned into the deserted parking lot. The sun was high in the sky. She grabbed her shotgun.

"Don't be stupid, Alessandra. No guns," a voice bellowed over a loudspeaker. "You've followed instructions so far. Come through the main doors. They're open."

With a curse, she tossed the weapon into the seat, resisting the urge to pat her ankle, where her knife rested.

"The blade, too," the voice roared. "You are trying my patience."

How could he possibly know?

A toddler's squeal sounded through the speaker. Lyssa didn't hesitate. She unstrapped the knife and removed the small pistol from her other ankle.

"Very good. You can be taught. I am pleased. Now walk through the front door."

Lyssa glanced around the parking lot. The gym loomed in front of her. A gust of frozen wind buffeted her. Somewhere, out of sight, Noah was there.

She wasn't alone. She had to believe that. She had to keep calm, keep cool and have faith in someone besides herself, a faith she'd lost two years ago. A faith she struggled to hold on to.

"Oh, Lyssa. Turn to the west. I have a surprise."

In the distance a huge explosion rocked the horizon. Fire and smoke billowed into the air.

"That was your two friends and their truck. I suggest you enter this building in the next fifteen seconds before I decide your daughter will receive *your* punishment for betraying me."

No. It couldn't be.

Black smoke burned. It was from the direction she'd come. Her entire body went numb. It wasn't possible. Noah couldn't be dead. Oh, God.

Her hands shook, her knees quivered. All she could see in her mind was Noah's ready smile, and his disappointed gaze.

She hadn't told him. She hadn't told him how she felt.

He'd given her everything, and she'd been too afraid to grab hold of what he offered. She'd done this. She'd caused his death. Now she was on her own, with Archimedes.

And her daughter.

She had to get ahold of herself. Remember what Noah had said. He'd believed in her. She could do this.

Lyssa shoved through the front door to the gym and skidded to a halt, stunned.

Silver-and-blue decorations littered the walls and ceiling. Balloons, streamers. It was as if the past ten years melted away.

Music played softly, Alicia Keys's "You Don't Know My Name."

In the center of the room, a red, strapless dress hung, a tiara and shoes to match on the floor below it. If it wasn't her prom dress, it was a close match.

A baby's scream echoed through the gym. It was quickly muffled.

Lyssa whirled around. "Don't hurt her. Please. I'll do anything you want!"

"I know you will," the silky voice echoed through the room.

A thin man dressed in a tuxedo walked through a curtain of streamers, a mask still covering his face. He stood several feet away from her.

"Two years. It's been two long years," he said with a smile. "You've run me a merry chase."

He watched her for a moment and Lyssa shivered under his study.

"You are more beautiful than ever. And you deciphered my message, which means you are my match." His arm swept around the gym. "Do you like it? This was how we were meant to fall in love."

A chill skittered down Lyssa's back at the singsong voice. She had no idea who he was. She only knew he had her daughter, and she had to be smart—smarter than Archimedes, smarter than she'd ever been in her life.

She clung to Noah's advice.

"I didn't understand," she said softly. "I'm sorry."

"I know, my dear." He stepped back. "Undress."

Lyssa couldn't move.

He crossed his arms. "Remove your clothes and put on the dress. Before I lose my patience."

He rubbed his temple. She didn't have a choice. Legs shaking, she walked over to the red gown, so very similar to the one from a decade ago. She touched the fabric then turned it to the back. She froze when she noticed the small tear near the zipper.

"Th-this is my dress." She staggered back. "H-how…?"

His smile widened. "You never noticed it disappeared from your closet, did you?"

She had, actually. She'd thought her mother gave it away. She'd been furious.

Archimedes circled her. "You danced with him all night.

Zeigler wasn't good enough for you." He spat out Bill's name. "He kissed you. He touched you."

"You were there?"

"I watched you push him away when he wanted to take you. I knew you were pure and innocent. I knew some- day you would be mine, that I would earn your respect. And your love.

"I have. The world knows my name."

Archimedes adjusted his tie. "Put on the dress."

Hands shaking, Lyssa lifted it off the hanger. "Is there a bathroom?" she asked. Maybe she could find a weapon, something to fight him with.

"No need for modesty, my dear. We will be together for eternity. Infinity and beyond. Remove your clothes."

His gaze bored into her. She turned away, trying to hide her bare breasts when she slipped the red satin over her head.

With the weight she'd lost the past couple of years, it still fit, though it was snug on her breasts and hips. Her body had changed.

Because of Jocelyn.

She would do this. For Jocelyn.

She removed her jeans and pushed them aside, then slipped into jewel-encrusted shoes. Frantically, she searched the gym for something, anything to use to fight him. There was nothing but balloons and streamers. What she wouldn't give for her gun or knife.

"Now the tiara," he said, his voice husky, his eyes heavy with want.

One glance told her this was no rhinestone tiara. These diamonds were real. Who was he?

She placed the crown on her head.

"Look at me," he whispered.

She faced him.

He smiled. "Just as I imagined."

She smoothed down the dress. "Can I see my baby now?" she pleaded. "Is she okay?"

He scowled at her. "She's not crying, is she? I'm the important one right now. Me. You will pay attention to *me*."

His fists clenched, his frown deepened. She'd messed up. She had to keep him calm. She had to keep him happy.

Oh, Noah. Now was when he was supposed to force his way into the gym and shoot Archimedes. That he didn't meant only one thing. Noah really was dead.

Mustering all the courage she could find within herself, she moved closer to him. She would stay alive, no matter what. She'd find a way out for her and her daughter.

Somehow. Someway.

Her body trembling, she stepped forward. "I'm sorry. You're right. What do you want me to do?"

He hit the button on a remote, switching to Norah Jones's "Come Away With Me." "Dance with me."

She hesitated, her gaze flitting to each corner of the room, searching for her daughter. His eyes grew hard. "No tricks, Alessandra. My little remote controls not only your life but your child's life, as well." He held out his hand. "Dance with me."

Music played over the speakers. She walked to Archimedes, the man who had killed Jack, her first love, the father of her child. The man who had killed Noah Bradford—Noah, who had restarted her heart.

She placed her hand in Archimedes's. He squeezed her, his touch firm yet strangely gentle. It was the first time he'd touched her, and she fought back the squirm. She let Archimedes hold her close when she wanted to bring her knee up and run.

She wouldn't risk Jocelyn's life. She couldn't chance it.

Lyssa followed his lead, her body stiff against his. His

breath hissed against her ear. "I knew we would fit together perfectly."

He grabbed her hands and placed them on his shoulders, pulling her close. His body brushed against hers. Nausea formed in the base of her throat.

A few blinks cleared tears from her eyes. She scanned the room, desperate to locate Jocelyn. She'd heard the cry. Her daughter had to be nearby.

"Please, can I see the baby?" she whispered in his ear.

He shoved her away from him. "You had to ruin it, didn't you? Asking for what you want, never thinking of my needs first." He clicked the remote. "You'll learn." The music stopped. A shiver went through Lyssa. Oh, God, what had she done?

Archimedes paced back and forth, then in larger circles as if his mind were a racetrack. Was he going to implode right there?

"It wasn't the plan," he muttered over and over again. He whirled on her. "Don't move." He raised the remote in the air, then walked across the gym to a closet. He pulled out a handkerchief, turned the doorknob then peeked inside. He disappeared for a moment, but soon dragged out a wooden chair and placed it in the middle of the floor. "Sit."

Lyssa had no choice. She sat down.

Within seconds he had bound her with nylon rope. Her hands and feet anchored together, he finished off with an elaborate knot.

"First we come to an understanding. Then I allow you to see your child."

He turned away from her, lifted his hands and slowly peeled away his mask.

Lyssa's heart raced. She would finally see him.

He faced her.

Archimedes, the serial killer feared by everyone, looked

like, like no one. Lyssa didn't know what she'd expected. Someone handsome like Ted Bundy. Someone odd like Jeremy Dahmer. This man was ordinary. Plain brown hair, plain brown eyes. No unusual features. He was nothing special. Forgettable really.

She blinked. And she had no idea who he was.

He leaned forward. His entire body thrummed with expectation, his expression eager, waiting.

God, she was supposed to know him.

Lyssa averted her gaze, desperately trying to piece together his identity. She'd only been at Thomas Jefferson for half of her senior year. Not enough time to make many friends—just Mary. Definitely not time to make enemies.

No one had stalked her; no one had harassed her.

His dress shoes thudded two steps. He grabbed her chin.

"You *must* know me," he said. His Adam's apple bobbed.

She licked her lips. What could she say? She studied his eyes, his hair. She bowed her head.

"What's my name?" he screamed.

She shook.

"Answer me!"

"I…I don't know. I'm sorry. Please, tell me."

He let out a wild cry. "You don't remember!" The accusation echoed in the gym. "Maybe *she'll* help you remember."

He raced across the gym to another door. The moment he slammed into the room, a baby's terrified cry sliced at Lyssa's soul.

He dragged a Pack 'n Play halfway across the room, the baby hysterical inside. Lyssa leaned forward, the rope bit into her arms and legs, but she didn't care. She had to get to Jocelyn.

Archimedes took a can and sprinkled powder all over

the playpen. He held a lighter above her baby. "The formula will incinerate her in seconds. Do you remember me now?"

Lyssa rocked back and forth. He was going to kill them both. She knew it. If she could knock the chair over and break the wood, maybe she could get free. "Please, please don't! I'll go with you. I won't fight you, just please leave her alone."

He shook his head, pacing again. "You are my destiny. We had something special. A moment. You cared. I know you did." He babbled, rubbing his temple. "That day at the UN, you didn't remember me then, either." He glared at her. "I thought you were different from the rest of them."

Lyssa strained her memory. Then, in a flash, she saw his face. The day of her big break, the translating job that would have made her career. A week before Jack's murder. Someone had stopped her, told her how proud he was of her. She'd ignored him. Pushed him aside.

"You congratulated me," she said softly.

He smiled a strange, sickly smile. "But you still don't know who I am."

"Maybe this will help." He removed a pair of thick glasses from his tuxedo pocket and put them on.

She struggled. She knew him. She had to. Someone out of place in high school. Someone the other kids didn't like.

Lyssa stared at his glasses. Yes. She remembered. A boy she hardly knew. He sat behind her in almost every class. Next to her in every class where they were assigned seating in alphabetical order. Alessandra Cummings then...

"Todd? Todd Davidson?"

The smartest kid in school. And the most awkward.

"I tested you and tested you." He sighed. "You figured out my puzzle. I thought we were meant to be together forever, that we'd have a life together. I guess I was wrong. Our lives will end together."

He sprinkled the powder around her.

"Please, don't do this. What did I ever do to you?"

"You made me believe people could be nice. Before you, I expected bullies to dump me into a garbage can. Before you, I expected teachers to ignore the bruises on my arms and legs and cheeks. Before you, I *expected* to disappear.

"You made me hope for more. You stood up for me." His face twisted in fury. "You made me love you!"

"Would it help if I told you that you do matter? Those things shouldn't have happened to you, Todd. They were wrong, but you don't have to do this." she said, desperation clawing at her. She had to get away. She shifted in her chair, tugging at the rope.

"You're too late. You don't know me!" he shouted. "You don't care about me! You never did. I made myself important. I am *Archimedes!*"

Jocelyn sobbed, stretching her hands out at Lyssa.

There had to be a way.

She looked on in horror as he sprinkled the powder along the perimeter of the building. He rambled, clutching his head in his hands. She couldn't make out what he was saying, but she could see what he was doing. She twisted her wrists, but the rope just cut into her more, tightening the grip on her legs.

He flicked his lighter and the powder exploded. A flame ripped up the wall of the gym. Todd smiled at the fire, staring into the heat.

"Our destiny, Alessandra. You and me. For infinity."

Chapter Thirteen

Thick smoke smothered Noah. Faraway sirens sounded somewhere in the distance. He rolled over onto his back, groaning. He blinked and looked up at the sky. "Lyssa." His charred voice cracked.

His head throbbed, and the memories flooded through him. The land mine. He'd seen it just in time. They'd jumped clear.

The SUV hadn't been so lucky The acrid scent of burning rubber seized his lungs. Fire still consumed the truck. He squinted through the billowing black fog.

A wheeze sounded from a few feet away. Noah crawled over to Elijah. He was hurt. Bad. The right side of his body had taken the worst of it. Noah pulled his phone from his pocket.

"Where are you?" He coughed when Ransom answered.

"Just landing in D.C."

"Archimedes caught us by surprise. Elijah's hurt. Need an ambulance." Noah gave Ransom the coordinates.

He struggled to his feet, sucking in deep breaths.

"Noah, are you there?" Ransom shouted.

Noah squeezed his eyes shut, then opened them, willing his vision to clear. He stumbled forward. In the distance, flames licked at the roof of a large building.

Lyssa!

"The gym is on fire, Ransom." He searched around for his weapon then cursed. It was now a melted chunk of metal. "I'm going in. Lyssa's alone."

"We're on our way."

He ended the call and bent over Elijah. "Buddy, can you hear me?"

Elijah opened his eyes and winced in pain, but not a sound escaped. "Ransom's on his way. I've got to go to her."

"Kill the bastard," Elijah hissed through clenched teeth. He closed his eyes and passed out.

Noah pressed his fingers against his carotid. Pulse barely there. He scrubbed his hands on his face. "Don't you die on me, Elijah."

He took off as fast as his burned leg would allow toward the gym, crossing a field. It took what seemed like forever to reach the main doors.

He yanked at them. They rattled, chained from the inside. There had to be another way.

He rounded the building. Two more sides, nothing but locked, barricaded doors. His head spun, but he shoved the weakness aside. Lyssa was depending on him.

Was she even inside?

He tugged his phone from his pocket and tapped an icon. About twenty feet away a small green dot blinked. Thank God for the coin he'd given her. At least he had a location.

Except, she wasn't moving.

One side left. He turned the corner. Finally. A small window halfway up the side of the gym gave him hope. Flames snaked from the roof, crackling. White smoke poured from the flames. No time to be picky. He was alone, and Lyssa was trapped.

He wouldn't allow himself to consider she was anything but alive.

Noah hauled himself by the small ledge. He smashed through the glass and heaved into the small space. His shoulders barely fit, but he shimmied through and dropped to the floor of a small closet.

His leg buckled, but he gritted through the pain.

Gaze half on the locator screen of his phone and half on his path, he opened the door to a hallway. He broke into a run to a set of large doors. That had to be the gym. Unnatural heat plowed into him with each step.

By the time he reached the doors, flames burst through the windows. He couldn't get through.

A loud crash sounded.

"Lyssa!"

With a quick scan, he sprinted to an equipment room. His hands touched the entrance. Cool to the touch. He burst inside.

Another door led out. He peered through its window.

The entire perimeter of the gym had been engulfed in flames. The fire devoured the streamers and decorations. A bevy of balloons exploded, sounding like a flurry of machine gun fire.

Surrounded by the inferno, in the center of the gym a man stood in a tuxedo over a downed chair. Lyssa lay on the floor at his feet, the chair broken, ropes slipped off.

They had a chance if Lyssa was conscious.

A child screeched above the roar of the fire. A playpen twenty feet away holding the screaming toddler.

Noah didn't waste any more time. He grabbed a uniform from the laundry basket and wrapped a shirt around his hand. He turned the knob. It gave way. Without a gun, he'd have to improvise. Basketballs, baseballs, footballs.

Too bad Chase wasn't here. He'd been an ace pitcher.

Noah grabbed three baseballs and slammed through the door. Without hesitation, he hurled a ball at Archimedes. It hit him in the center of his back.

"What the hell?"

Archimedes spun around. Lyssa scrambled away from the broken chair toward her baby. Archimedes dived at her, grabbing her by the ankle.

Noah threw another ball. This time it was a direct hit in the head.

Archimedes slumped to the ground, groaning.

Lyssa crawled to the screaming baby.

The flames hit the center of the roof. Smoke thickened around them, metal creaked. A section of ceiling started to peel away. Noah launched himself toward Jocelyn, grabbing the toddler out of the Pack 'n Play. Shifting to his back, he slid across the floor, Lyssa's daughter in his arms.

The ceiling crushed the playpen.

Noah held Jocelyn close.

"You're alive." Lyssa started toward him.

Archimedes rolled onto his back. "It's not you. It can't be you. You're in Denver." He stood, swaying, and clutched the remote to his chest. "You'll pay!"

He flicked a switch and smiled. "Say goodbye to your sister." He lifted a tablet computer showing a building collapsing.

Lyssa didn't hesitate. "You bastard!" She ran at Todd, head-butting him with all her strength.

Archimedes skidded toward a wall. Noah handed a screaming Jocelyn to Lyssa. "Can you run?"

Above them beams split. Ashes rained over them.

"Duck!" Noah shouted.

She covered Jocelyn while Noah grabbed Archimedes by the collar.

The man laughed in his face. "She's mine. I took her from her fiancé, I'll take her from you. She'll die by my side!"

He reached into his pocket, pulling out a knife. He swiped at Noah.

"Hell, no."

In a practiced move, Noah twisted Archimedes's arm behind his back. "You'll pay for what you've done. I promise you that," he hissed in his ear.

A beam crashed right beside them, sparks flying.

"Get out, Lyssa," he shouted. "Now!"

She stumbled to her feet. "There's no way out!"

"We'll die together," Archimedes chuckled. "All you had to do was love me."

Just then an SUV rammed through the front of the gym. Ransom and two other men jumped out. "Go! The place is coming down."

The car backed out, leaving a gaping hole. Lyssa clutched Jocelyn and ran through. Noah held Archimedes firm.

"Move it," he said rushing Archimedes through the door. To Noah's left side a wall crashed down, barely missing them. Shrapnel pummeled over them, fiery weapons. One grazed his arm, setting his jacket ablaze.

He shucked it to the ground, and Archimedes broke free. He raced back into the gym.

"Stop," Noah shouted.

"You'll never take me."

A huge creaking noise erupted from the walls and ceiling. Archimedes turned and stared, his jaw open wide, stunned.

Half the wall fell on top of, burying him in flames.

He'd killed himself.

NOAH PEERED INTO the burning gym.

Archimedes was gone. Dead.

Fire truck sirens filled the air. Lyssa walked over to Noah, carrying Jocelyn.

"What are you doing out of the SUV?" He put his arm

around her, propping her up as she cuddled the baby in her arms.

"Are you hurt?"

Smoke poured from what remained of the gym. She coughed and yanked the tiara off her head. "I'm fine."

"What are you wearing?" Noah asked.

"It was my high school prom dress. I thought my mom gave it away. He stole it."

"Who was he?"

"Todd Davidson, a kid from my class."

"Why did he do this, Lyssa?"

She rocked Jocelyn, praying the little girl would fall asleep. "I don't know," she said, her voice lowered. "The thing is, I only talked to him once. Some jocks were bullying them. I told them to stop. That was it. He turned it into some twisted love affair."

Jocelyn whimpered. Lyssa jostled the baby and told Noah everything Todd had said in the gym.

Noah touched the baby's soft skin. She looked so much like Lyssa.

Ransom walked over to them. "The second ambulance is en route." He held out his hand to Lyssa. "I'm Ransom Grainger. Good to meet you and I'm glad you're okay."

"Lyssa…" She hesitated and looked over at Noah.

"It's over. Use whichever name you prefer."

"Alessandra doesn't exist anymore. I like Lyssa."

Noah gave her a quick smile. "Lyssa suits you," he said. "I've gotten used to it." He turned to Ransom. "How's Elijah?"

"Not great, but he'll make it. By the way, Reid's out of the coma. He's asking for both of you."

"Tell him Archimedes is dead. Tell him everything," Noah said.

"Marmie?" Jocelyn stared at Ransom, then at Noah, then finally at Lyssa. Her lip trembled. "Marmie?"

"Do you have a phone?" Lyssa asked Noah.

He pulled it out of his pocket. Lyssa quickly went to a cloud account she'd purchased under Jack's mother's maiden name and prayed Mary hadn't changed the password.

She clicked on the link.

A video started playing.

Jocelyn's ears perked up. She clutched the phone and stared.

"Mama!" she said, smiling. The little girl hummed along to "Hush, Little Baby."

Noah leaned over her shoulder. It was Lyssa singing to the baby. A slightly younger Lyssa, her face had been a bit fuller, but it was her.

"Mama!" The baby hugged the phone to her.

A tear slid down Lyssa's cheek. "Mary showed her the video. I knew she would."

Noah stood solidly behind her quietly while the baby watched.

"Marmie?" she questioned.

"She's not here, baby." Lyssa kissed the little girl's cheek. "Mama's here, though. I love you."

Jocelyn's chin quivered. She looked confused.

"It'll take time," Noah whispered.

"This wasn't how it was supposed to be," Lyssa said. "Mary wasn't supposed to die. No one was."

Ransom walked over, holding out a phone. "It's Rafe," he said.

Noah grabbed it. "Tell me you got her out!"

Lyssa leaned into the phone.

"Barely. Zane broke through the signal just in time.

The damn building exploded as we were leaving, but I got her out."

"Can I talk to her?"

"She's in the E.R.," Rafe said, his voice exhausted. "She won't say what he did to her, but she's a fighter."

"Take care of her. I'll be home as soon as I clear up a few details." He listened. "Yeah, home to stay. I want to be part of the family again. No more secrets."

Lyssa stilled. She was a detail to be cleared up, then he'd be leaving. She hadn't considered... She should have realized...

She held Jocelyn closer. Lyssa's life had to be about what was best for her daughter. She had Jocelyn; Noah had his family. They needed him.

"The ambulance is here," Ransom said.

Noah wrapped his arm around her shoulders. "Let's get you and Jocelyn checked out."

Lyssa fought against her own needs. She had to stay strong. "We can go ourselves. You should see to your family." She blinked, forcing back the emotions threatening to overwhelm her.

Noah stilled. "Is that what you want?"

No. But she couldn't say the words. "It's best." She'd caused him enough heartache. Why wouldn't he want to leave?

She crawled into the back of the ambulance with Jocelyn. The paramedic placed oxygen masks on her and the baby.

The driver closed the door and they sped down the road.

Ransom walked over to Noah and slapped him upside the head. "What the hell are you doing?"

"She...she told me to go."

"You might be the best agent I've got, Falcon. You might be able to read the enemy like a damn psychic, but you're an idiot when it comes to women. That woman practically begged you to go with her."

Noah shook his head. "You're wrong. Now that it's over…"

"Now that it's over, nothing is stopping her from letting down her guard."

He stared at the white van as it disappeared behind a small hill.

"Everything happened too fast. What feelings she has—if they're still there—probably aren't real. Not like…" his voice trailed off. He'd nearly said, "not like mine."

"You ever felt this way before?" Ransom asked.

"I loved the idea of her the moment I met her," Noah admitted, staring at the ground. "She's more than I dreamed of. She smart, determined, fierce, brave—"

"Then what are you doing standing here? Afraid?"

"Terrified. She might realize her feelings for me are only based on gratitude."

"Been there, done that, Noah. Let me share something my wife taught me. Don't assume anything about a woman's feelings. Because more often than not, we don't give them enough credit. Trying to protect her, I almost lost my wife. Don't let Lyssa get away." Ransom dropped a set of keys into Noah's hand. "Go get her. If she turns you down, I'll have a bottle of whiskey on the plane waiting for you."

Noah clutched the keys. "If she turns me down, I'll need it."

It took twenty minutes to locate the hospital where they'd taken Lyssa. Noah strode into the E.R. "Lyssa Cafferty?" he asked.

"Family?" the nurse asked.

"I hope so," he said quietly.

She sent him a harsh frown. "If you're why that young lady is crying behind curtain three, you better get in there and beg for her forgiveness." The woman crossed her arms over her ample bosom and glared at him.

He swallowed. "Yes, ma'am."

If the men who'd placed the Falcon on the most wanted list in Afghanistan had seen Noah's tentative tug of the curtain, they'd have laughed their asses off.

"Lyssa?"

He entered the small curtained-off room. She swiped her hand over her face, but her eyes were red, her cheeks tear-stained.

"Where's Jocelyn?"

"They took her for an X-ray. They wouldn't let me go." She dug her fists into the blanket. "What are you doing here?"

He crossed the room and sat in the chair beside the bed. "Are you okay?"

"A few bruises from knocking the chair over and breaking it so I could hit the deck." She held out her wrists. "The rope cut into my skin. Otherwise, I'm fine. What are you doing here? I thought you were going home."

He stared up into her eyes, trying to read her emotions, trying to control the swirl of want inside of him. Should he tell her how he felt? He wanted to, but his entire body shook with apprehension. He'd faced death more times than he cared to admit, but he'd never been truly afraid until this moment.

She could destroy him.

He covered her hand with his. "I couldn't leave. I had to be sure—"

She wouldn't meet his gaze. "I'm fine. Jocelyn will be fine. I'll make sure she knows what an amazing woman raised her for the first two years of her life. We'll be f-fine," she stammered.

He grabbed her hands. "I know you will. That's the

thing, Lyssa. You'll be fine on your own. I have no doubt about that. You don't need me. But I—"

She leaned forward. "What are you trying to say?"

"I want you," he rushed out. "I know it's too soon. I know you still love Jack, but I want to be part of your life. I…I love you, Lyssa Cafferty."

He squeezed her hands until she winced. Cursing, he let her go.

"I'm sorry." He turned away. "This was a mistake."

"Noah," she said softly. "I love you, too."

He spun around, afraid to hope, afraid her big heart was lying to her, but he couldn't stop himself from tucking her into his arms and sitting down on the chair with her in his lap. His hands gentle, he kissed her slowly, reverently, and pressed his closed eyes against her shoulder, unwilling to admit the burn behind his eyelids was anything other than the residual effect of the fire and smoke.

"Are you sure?" his voice choked out. "We've been through a lot. It might not be—"

"Don't say it isn't real, Noah. I know what I feel. You're brilliant, you're determined, you're the man I fell in love with. All of you. All your masks. The Falcon, Noah Bradford, CEO, but mostly, I just love you, the man, Noah."

His smile broadened and he lowered his lips. Her mouth parted under his. His body surged with desire until they heard a toddler squealing.

A harried orderly walked into the room and thrust her at Lyssa. "She's all yours. Nothing wrong with her lungs."

Tears fell down Jocelyn's face. Lyssa stood and held out her arms, but the little girl pulled away. "Marmie. I want Marmie!"

Noah couldn't bear the crying. He took Jocelyn into his strong arms and bounced her a bit. "What are those tears for, pumpkin pie?"

The orderly gulped in relief and rushed away.

Noah lifted Jocelyn in the air. Her green eyes—so like her mother's—stared down at him, then she smiled and giggled. After a few more soars into the air, he pulled her into his arms and sat down next to the bed.

Lyssa touched Jocelyn's hair. "Mama loves you, baby girl."

Jocelyn blinked her eyes, settling her head against Noah's shoulder.

He smiled, holding the small body as gently as he could. "She's going to have me wrapped around her finger in no time."

"Me, too." Lyssa risked a look at him. "She could use a good man in her life."

"One man?" Noah asked. "Would you settle for one man, Lyssa? Me, the man who loves you, who runs his companies, who stays home and doesn't live an exciting life?"

"What about the Falcon?" Lyssa asked. "Won't you miss it."

"The Falcon is dead," Noah said. "I think it's time I remind myself who I am and hang up the adventures for a while. Besides, I have a feeling you and this little lady will provide plenty of adventure for me."

Rows of white crosses dotted the military cemetery. A nip of cold brought a chill to the winter air, but Noah didn't feel it. Lyssa's joyous smile warmed him from the inside.

When they'd pulled Archimedes's body from the remains of the gym, he'd finally seen that little line on her forehead smooth completely away. Until that moment, somewhere in her mind she'd wondered if he was still out there.

The nightmare was over. Archimedes was dead.

Now they had one more goodbye.

Lyssa placed a small photo on top of the cross. She laid her hand reverently on the stone. Part of Noah winced. Would she ever love him the way she'd loved Jack? For now, he'd just accept what she said, but he had to admit he doubted. She and Jack had been perfect together, but Noah wasn't Jack.

He couldn't pretend to be.

She walked over to the car with Jocelyn. The toddler didn't smile much but clung to Lyssa.

"You ready?" Noah asked, opening the back door for her so she could put Jocelyn in her car seat.

She nodded. "Thank you for bringing me here."

"You okay?"

Lyssa smiled up at him and gripped his fingers, squeezing tight. "Yeah. We have Jocelyn back. We're safe. Jack would like that."

After she'd put Jocelyn into the car seat, Noah opened the passenger door. Lyssa scooted inside out of the wind.

Noah paused, glancing at the gravestone. "Give me a minute?" he asked.

Her gaze quizzical, she nodded.

Slowly, he walked to the lone cross and stared down at the name.

Jackson David Holden.

His chest tightened with emotion, filling his chest and heart. Hope and more fear than he wanted to admit. "You were a lucky man, Jack. I wish I had been there that day, more than you know, but she's safe now. You'd be proud of her. Man, she's a hell of a fighter."

He swiped at the bit of dirt at the base of the cross. "You have an amazing daughter, my friend. That little girl is just like her mom. Beautiful, smart, funny. And stubborn. She tells you what she wants and doesn't let go until she gets it." He rubbed the base of his neck. "She's got your charm, too. I'm in so much trouble when the boys start coming around. I'll take good care of her. Of both of them. I promise you that. Until the day I die."

A swirl of hope pushed Noah to his knees. "I thank God every day for them, Jack. I'm sorry she lost you. I'm sorry you lost her, but I love them both with all my heart and soul. I don't know if she'll ever love me as much as she loved you, I'll probably always be second best but I'll take what I can get. A little piece of her heart is worth the world."

He pressed his fingers to his eyes, straightened his shoulders and turned around. Shocked he hadn't heard her walk up behind him, Noah flushed.

Lyssa stood behind him, her eyes wet with tears, and Jocelyn in her arms. She gripped his shirt collar and pulled him to her. "You listen to me, Noah Bradford. I loved Jack. I'll always love him and remember him, but you, you hold my heart. Jack loved the woman I was. You accept the woman I became. The woman I am now." She brought his head close to hers. "You healed my heart, Noah. I never thought I'd believe in love again. I need you with everything in me. Believe that. Believe in me."

He wrapped his arms around her and Jocelyn and pulled them close. His body trembled. "I want to, but won't you always wish for what might have been. How can I compete with a memory?"

"You don't have to."

She pulled his head down to hers and took his lips in a kiss. The passion in her touch tugged at his heart. "I admire the man who was smart enough and strong enough to stop the man who killed Jack. I need the man who holds me in his arms each night. I adore the man who took Jocelyn into his arms and quieted her when she cried. I cherish the man who even now checks on her in the middle of the night when he thinks I'm still asleep.

"And I love the man standing in front of me with all my heart. I love *you,* Noah Bradford. And I always will."

"I love you, Lyssa. I'll always love you." Noah tightened his hold, the fear in his heart melting when she placed her head on his shoulder. Together they walked to the car.

He opened the door.

"Da!" Jocelyn yelled when he got in.

He stared at Lyssa. She grinned. "She learned a new word. Guess she knows who you are."

He leaned over and kissed Lyssa's lips tenderly, then ruffled Jocelyn's hair.

"Let's go home, family."

Epilogue

Noah drove up to his father's Denver ranch house. It looked the same as it had a week ago. Of course, Noah's life was completely different now.

He rounded the car and opened the door for Lyssa. She hesitated. "Are you sure they're not angry with me? I stopped you from coming home."

Noah unbuckled Jocelyn from her car seat and pulled the chatterbox into his arms. "Sierra is safe. That's all that matters. They understand."

Still, Lyssa paused.

"Hey, it's my family. I love you, they will, too. Besides, you've got me staying in Denver most of the time. They like that. A lot."

Holding her hand, he strode up the stairs and gave three short knocks.

His sister stood in the doorway, smiling at him. "It's about time!" He studied her face. Her cheek was scraped and her arm was in a sling. There was a haunted look in her eyes he understood but didn't like. She should never have been taken.

Sierra turned to Lyssa. "I'm so glad to meet you." His sister pulled Lyssa into her arms.

"I'm so sorry." Tears filled Lyssa's eyes. "It's my—"

"Don't say it." Sierra waved the apology away. "He was

a nut job. I'm glad he's dead." Even then, Noah noted the tremor in his sister's hand.

After a gulp of wine, Sierra tilted her head. "I heard he left a list of all his so-called sacrifices. Way more than anyone knew."

"How'd you figure that out?" Noah asked.

"It's not like you'll brag," Sierra said. "I had to find out through the grapevine that the code you deciphered from his crazy symbols opened a safe where he kept a record of everything he'd done. You guys make quite the team."

Lyssa looked up at him. "Yeah, we do."

They entered the Bradford home. The wooden floors gleamed, and Paul wheeled over to them. "So, you finally brought her here." He smiled at Lyssa. "Thank you," he said, holding out his hands.

She reached out to him, a furrow of confusion on her brow. "I don't understand."

"You gave me back my son."

Paul looked up at Jocelyn. "And who might this be?"

Jocelyn tilted her head at Paul, then she grinned and held out her arms, wiggling toward him. Noah maneuvered the baby into his father's arms. Paul laughed and set her on his knee. "Want to go for a ride, little lady?"

She giggled and Paul wheeled them around the room.

"Where's everyone else?" Noah asked, taking Lyssa's hand in his and giving her a slight squeeze. She smiled up at him, even while keeping an eye on her daughter.

"Mitch and Emily will be here soon," Sierra said. "Emily's only two weeks away from delivery, so they're a little slow getting out of the gate sometimes. Chase is on his way."

Noah took Lyssa's coat and hung it up. His shoulders tingled. He turned. Rafe stood in the door of the kitchen. Noah strode over to him. "Thank you."

Rafe nodded, but as usual said nothing.

"How'd you find her?"

Rafe scowled at Sierra. "You might want to ask your sister."

She rolled her eyes. "Oh, for God's sake."

"I'm not leaving until you tell everyone." He crossed his arms. The tension between them crackled.

"What's going on?"

"Your sister isn't just an accountant," Rafe scowled. "She's working for CTC. You know the ace forensic accountant Ransom tapped for special jobs. It's Sierra."

"What?" Noah shouted.

Jocelyn whimpered from Paul's lap, her lower lip sticking out.

Noah quickly knelt in front of them. "Sorry, babycakes." He blew a raspberry on her tummy until she smiled again then glared at Sierra. "How long?"

"A few years," Sierra said with a death stare aimed at Rafe. "It's a good thing I had the training, too. I knocked that door cockeyed just enough you noticed it. Otherwise, you wouldn't have found me."

"I was in the damn building."

"Yeah, when it exploded."

Rafe growled under his breath. "I'm out of here, Noah. Talk some sense into her or get her fired."

He disappeared through the kitchen and Sierra flopped onto the couch. "Good riddance."

Noah stared down at her. "Why the secrets?"

Sierra shot him a disbelieving look. "You're one to talk."

"She's right." Lyssa sidled up beside Noah.

He rubbed his chin. "I know. But you'll give Ransom your resignation."

She shrugged.

"Sierra—"

"It's my life to live, big brother. You can't control everything."

Lyssa turned to Noah and grinned, then kissed him.

Noah lingered a little bit before pulling away. "What are you smiling at?"

Paul chuckled. "She's got your number, Noah. You done good." He looked down at Jocelyn. "Want a cookie, little lady?"

"Cookie!" Jocelyn squealed.

Paul wheeled them into the kitchen. Sierra stood in the corner of the room, looking out the window. Lyssa shoved him toward her.

He sighed and walked over to Sierra. "I'm sorry, sis. I know what working for CTC means. You must be damn good at your job for Ransom to take you on. But..." He hesitated. "It can eat away at your soul. Just be careful."

"I am." She looked up at him. "Do you regret what you've done?"

"I have regrets. There are things I saw that...well, let's just say I'll never forget." He glanced over at Lyssa. "But they gave me the means to stop Archimedes. So, no."

Sierra tilted her head. "You kept it a secret. You must know why I did."

"I'm going to slug Ransom when I see him."

"I made him promise," Sierra countered.

"Well, the secrets are out in the open now." Noah looked toward the kitchen where his friend had left. "Sierra, be careful of Rafe. He doesn't let anyone in."

"I know," she said sadly. "I tried that already." She walked across the room and poked at the fire.

Noah bristled and started toward her. Lyssa stepped into his path and clutched his arm. "Don't," she whispered, meeting his gaze. "She cares about him."

"He can't give her what she needs."

"And you can't convince her of that, Noah." Lyssa nodded her head. "Look at her."

A shout sounded from outside. "Open the door!" Chase yelled.

Chase carried a huge turkey with both hands. "Happy Thanksgiving."

Mitch followed, his arm protectively around Emily as she waddled up the ramp with her son in her arms.

Both brothers engulfed Lyssa in bear hugs.

"So, bro, someone finally tamed you." Chase chuckled.

Emily swatted at him and set down Joshua. "Just you wait, Chase."

"Oh, no. I like my life just how it stands, thank you very much."

Chaos ensued. By the time dinner was on the table, Noah stepped back for a moment and simply watched. For the first time in so many years, he relished the chuckles, with no need to hide what he said or lie about what he'd done.

His siblings needled each other diving for the last helping of sweet-potato pie. Mitch constantly watched out for Emily. Jocelyn and Joshua giggled as first one of his brothers and then the other lifted the toddlers across the table to fight over the turkey leg.

Noah slipped something from his pocket and placed it on a wishbone. He leaned back. Chase met his gaze then grinned.

Lyssa was deep in conversation with Emily. She hadn't seen what he'd done.

"Can I borrow her, Emily?" Noah asked, suddenly nervous. "Want to help me clear the table?" He picked up the turkey.

She smiled. "Of course."

She followed her in and he set down the platter. Noah

clutched Lyssa's hand and pulled her aside. "What do you think?"

She smiled up at him. "You have an amazing family. And I think Jocelyn is in love with Joshua." The two kids held hands throughout dinner, when they weren't covered in mashed potatoes.

He cleared his throat and then swallowed, his nerves nearly shot. "I have a special family tradition I wanted to share with you," he said, reaching for the wishbone.

He looked up. The entire family stood in the kitchen doorway watching.

"Da!" Jocelyn shouted, stretching out her arms. He snagged the little girl. "Want to see if your wish comes true?"

Lyssa reached out and stared at the red ribbon attached to the wishbone.

Hanging off the silk was a diamond ring. An engagement ring.

He knelt down. "Would you be a part of the Bradford family, Lyssa? I love you. I promise I'll do whatever it takes to make you and Jocelyn happy."

She stared at the ring, then up at him.

"I love you, Noah Bradford. The one and only." She smiled at him. "Of course, I'll marry you."

The entire family erupted in cheers.

A glass of champagne later and Paul wheeled into the corner with Jocelyn and Joshua in his lap.

Thanksgiving had officially come, and they had a lot to be thankful for.

Noah tucked Lyssa close to him and kissed her temple. She turned in his arms. "It's forever, right?"

"Forever and always."

* * * * *

REQUEST YOUR FREE BOOKS!
2 FREE NOVELS PLUS 2 FREE GIFTS!